RIDING HARD FOR A THUG 2

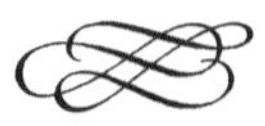

NIKKI BROWN

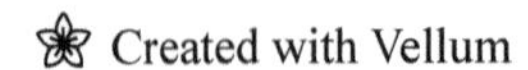
Created with Vellum

K.C. MILLS PRESENTS

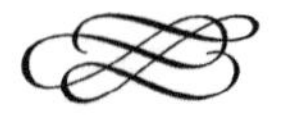

RIDING HARD FOR A THUG 2

By: Nikki Brown

ASTA

Where we left off…

The minute I saw Wolf walk off the elevator with Simon I knew shit was about to hit the fan. I didn't think he was gonna out me like that, but then again no one knew about Simon in the bike world, and that's how I wanted to keep it.

Although Simon was calm as hell, the look in his eyes was a little scary. We had fought a time or two but nothing too serious. Don't get me wrong I could hold my own, but in this situation, I thought it best that I leave and go to my sister's house. I wasn't in the mood to argue and fight with Simon, we both needed a while to cool down.

He didn't think I noticed the little exchanges between him and Ms. Hannah. She's the one that calls him all the time. When he told her to hold his appointments, she sounded extra desperate to keep him there. Something was up with that, he had questions for me, hell I had some for him too.

"Ne?" I answered the phone on the first ring.

"How did your interview go? You said you were gonna call me when you got out," she said all in one breath. There was so much going on right now that I forgot to call.

"Girl," I stopped at a stop light and threw my head against the head rest and closed my eyes for a second. "Today has been a bitch." The person behind me blew the horn letting me know that the light had turned green, normally I would cuss them the hell out, but right now I had too much on my mind.

"Are you okay?"

"No, I'm not, I'm coming to your house. I have to go home and get clothes first."

"Asta what the hell is going on you talking in circles." Neala fussed.

"Well first off, I met Hannah." I paused to wait for her reaction.

"And?"

"You were right, she's white, and there is definitely something going on." I sighed.

"Okay, And?"

"What do you mean and?"

"Girl, you spent the weekend with fine ass Ky, and he gave yo ass some act right, so please tell me why you worried about Simon's ass?"

"You're right." She was right the weekend I had with Ky had

me wanting to throw away my whole relationship with Simon. I had never felt the way I did this weekend, not emotionally and damn sure not sexually. "Speaking of fine ass Ky." I rolled my eyes like she could see me.

"Ah hell, please don't tell me I gotta cut his sexy ass."

"Can you chill on the compliments." I rolled my eyes again.

"Yo ass rolling yo eyes hard as hell, I can hear that shit through the phone." She laughed, and so did I.

"So, you remember Wolf right from the party?"

"Yeah."

"Well he was at Simon's office today, and when he saw me, he started asking about Ky and talking about how we looked like we were made for each other and shit girl right in front of Simon. That nigga was mad as hell."

"Wait hold the hell up, what was Wolf doing at Simon's office and what were you doing there. You never go there."

"Right, he called talking about we needed to talk, and he wanted me to stop by. I still don't know what the hell Wolf was doing there. I didn't even know they knew each other."

"You done got caught the fuck up."

"Hell yeah, Simon asking about who Ky was and all that. I just left, and now he wanna talk when he gets home."

"You need me to come over there?"

"Nah I think I'll be okay. I'll call you if I need you. I'm hoping that I can get in and get out before he even gets there. He looked like he was gone have to explain some stuff to his little girlfriend."

"Be careful Asta and call me either way, if I don't hear

anything from you within 20 minutes. I'm calling Ky, and we're one way."

"I'll call you girl."

I pulled into the drive way and jumped out. I threw my phone in my back pocket and ran in the house. I went into the closet and grabbed my black Nike bag and started throwing stuff in there. I had made it through my closets, it wasn't until I went to the bathroom to get my hygiene product that I heard him come into the house.

"Fuck!" I cursed myself for taking so long.

"Where the hell do you think you're going, Asta." He snatched my bag and threw it across the room, and I stopped what I was doing and talked myself out of punching him in the fucking face.

"I need a break Simon and from the looks of things so do you." I tried a softer approach.

"Why, so you can go lay-up with your little biker thug? What's his name Ky?" The evil smirk on his face was starting to bother me. "I bet you didn't think when you came into my office today your whole little affair would be exposed."

"My affair wasn't the only one exposed."

"So, you admit it?"

"What? I ain't admitting to shit, Ky is just a really good friend." I wasn't lying, Ky was a good friend that could fuck me into a coma, but he was a friend. "He's just someone I can talk to, especially about my career and he has thrown some great opportunities my way."

"So, *you fucking for fame now Asta?"*

"Simon, *you sound so fucking stupid."*

"That's what it sounds like to me."

"I didn't have to fuck him for him to care about my career, unlike you who don't give a fuck about anyone but yourself," I yelled. He was pissing me off. I was about to tell him what he wanted to hear and invite his ass to exit my life stage left.

"Oh, *this has nothing to do with me, so where were you this past weekend?"*

"In Farmington."

"With who?"

"My sister Simon got damn, I'm not about to sit here and play 20 questions with you."

"You will if I fucking say you are." He got in my face and pushed him away from me, and he laughed.

I can honestly say I had never seen him like this and I wasn't comfortable being here with him like this. I grabbed my phone to shoot my sister a text, but he snatched it away from me. I tried to get it back, and he pushed me so hard I fell. I could hear a text come through and I prayed that it wasn't Ky.

"How's my angel?" Simon read the text out loud. "Angel huh? I thought y'all were just friends?" he looked at me and then threw my phone over my head, and it hit the wall and shattered. "My father told me to stop fucking with you, he said that you weren't shit but a fucking hood rat *that would never amount to anything." He seethed and with every word he spoke I got even more pissed. "You were never good enough for me, and now I see that. You can get your shit and get the fuck out. Hannah is a better fit for me anyway."*

"I'm glad you think that, please go on with your Barbie I'm good on you. We've out grown each other anyway. I hope you happy with her and as far as your bitch ass father, tell him to take that big ass stick out his ass and he would see that not everybody was born to kiss ass." I threw back.

"I don't see what I saw in you."

"Ky sees a lot in me," I said getting up off the floor. I knew I should have stopped right there and not indulge in this little pissing match with him. Something about his words pissed me off, and I wanted him to feel like I felt at that moment. "He see's, even more, when he's looking me in the eyes as he makes love to me over and over and over again. That man does things to me that you have never been able to do. So, *all this shit." I waved my hands around the room. "Don't mean shit to me and what you just said, motivated me more to get the fuck up out of here," I yelled at him.*

He didn't say anything at first, he just stood there breathing, he wasn't even looking at me he was just zoned out. I took that as my chance to get the fuck out of there. I tried to run past him, but he grabbed me around the throat and lifted me off of my feet. I was struggling to breathe, he spun me around and threw me into the wall and that shit hurt like hell. He still had his hands around my throat.

I clawed at his hands, and he just stared at me. I tried my best to get him to loosen his grip but he wouldn't. I kicked and kicked and still nothing. I could feel the tears running down my face. My eyes started to get really heavy, it was becoming harder and harder to keep them open. I reached out to try and claw his face, but his arms were extended and much longer than mine. I said a quick prayer and prepared to take my last breath. I looked him in his eyes one more time, and then everything faded to black.

KY'SIER "KY" BRASHER

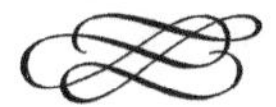

"Man, I don't know what the fuck to do, she wont even fucking talk to me." Rondo complained. I just looked at him because I didn't know what the fuck he wanted me to do, I told his dumb ass to tell her when he told me. The muthafucka didn't listen so he had to deal with this shit. "You hear what I just said nigga." He stopped pacing and stared at me.

I stopped cleaning my bike. "I heard you nigga. I told yo ass to tell her and you thought you had shit under control so now you gotta deal with that shit." I gave it to him raw and uncut, I wouldn't do that shit any other way.

"Yo ass trying to be Casanova and shit." Zan said walking to the front of the shop from the back office.

"Fuck you nigga." Rondo threw out.

"Fuck you ol' whining ass nigga." Zan laughed.

"Now is not the time for this shit. I need some advice." He threw himself down in the chair.

"Nigga go apologize and tell the truth." I gave him the simplest answer that I could think of I mean shit, it couldn't be that hard.

"It ain't gone be that easy Ky, you know we been trying to have kids and she keep losing em so hearing I might have another bitch pregnant is fucking with her."

I couldn't even say anything there because I had never been in that situation so I couldn't say how shit would go one way or another. I hoped shit worked out for them though, I looked up to their relationship. if they couldn't make it all hope was gone in my book. And that fucked with me because I was thinking long and hard about making shit right with Asta. I knew she was with that punk ass nigga but that was about to come to an end sooner than she knew.

"You betta get on your knees and eat ha ass nigga, you fucked up big time." Zan said and Rondo jumped up, I ran to get in between the two of them. I could tell that Rondo was starting to get pissed and this could get bad. Zan had a smart ass mouth and he didn't give a fuck if you were going through some shit or not he was gone say what the fuck he wanted to say.

"I'm out!" Rondo said as he knocked my hand down and walked out of the shop. I understood that he was pissed off but he was mad at the wrong muthafuckas.

We watched as he jumped on his bike and peeled out of the

parking lot. I shook my head and went back to fucking with my bike. I pulled out my phone to text Asta again. I had text her a few times in the last 20 minutes and I hadn't heard shit back. That girl kept that phone in her got damn hands so I'm sure she got my messages. I was convinced that her ass slept with it in her had.

This past weekend with Asta was one that I won't forget. I'ma thug ass nigga, and I've had my share of bitches so for someone to leave an impression on me meant something and that's why I planned on making her a more permanent fixture in my life.

"Knock knock muthafucka." I looked up and there was Wolf. I forgot his ass told us that he was coming up here this week to look at spaces for a shop.

"My nigga." I dapped him up.

"I swear you wipe anymore on that fucking bike the bitch gone be paintless and rusted." He laughed. I did clean my bike a lot but that shit calmed me and it was habit, that was my bitch and I was proud of it.

"Shut the fuck up." I laughed and he joined me.

"Aye I seen ya shorty today." He said and I looked at him confused and then it clicked that he meant Asta, we had a brief conversation after the Biker's Ball about her and her DJ skills. I told him that I was gone try and make her my shorty. "She acted like shit wasn't good."

"Where you see her at?"

"I went to check out this big real estate nigga named Simon, look like she was walking out while I was coming in." he gave me a questioning look. "I asked where you were and she down played y'all shit, so I was like, that ain't what I seen." He laughed and dapped me up. "Ol' boy didn't seem too happy about that shit."

"She ain't my girl yet, that was her nigga." I shrugged.

"Oh shit!" he put his fist to his mouth because he realized her just outed the fuck out of Asta. I didn't give a damn that shit gave me the opening that I needed. I hoped he got pissed and left her ass so I could swoop in and get my girl. Yeah, that's some bitch shit, but after this weekend a nigga was just gone take that shit. "Damn I didn't mean to do her like that."

"She'll be alright I had plans on telling her to let that shit go anyway."

"Calm the fuck down Neala," Zan yelled into his phone. I forgot that his ass was standing there for a minute. "Why the hell you just now telling some got damn body." He fussed. His face was all screwed up. "Yo Ky, Asta, and that bitch nigga got into it, and she was worried and shit about going home, Neala told her if she ain't heard from her in 20 minutes that she was coming. Said her sister called and when she answered she could hear them yelling in the background and now she can't get a hold of her."

"Where she at?" I didn't give a fuck about anything else the only thing on my mind was to find out where she was and make sure that she was okay.

"Where the hell she live?" Zan asked and listened to her response. When his face started contorting I knew she was on that bullshit. "Do you think we give a fuck about that bullshit, tell us where the hell she is so we can make sure she aight." She said something else, and he hung up the phone without responding. "Talking about she don't want us to go because we will make shit worse. Fuck that they stay over in Crossover." He said pointing in the direction of the housing development that was about five minutes from the shop.

I nodded, and we took off leaving Wolf there questioning where we were going. I didn't have time to answer his questions; I needed to get to Asta I would feel fucked up if something happened to her on the strength of me. I knew how niggas could be and I didn't want that for her.

We jumped in my Charger and sped over to the Crossover development; we didn't know what house because Zan's temperamental ass wouldn't wait for her to tell us. We drove around for a couple of minutes before I spotted her car. I automatically knew something was wrong when I noticed the door wide open.

"I swear fo God if he put his hands on her I'ma fucking kill that nigga." I gritted not really directing my comment at anyone.

"Chill bro," Zan said making his way to the door. He had his piece on him as usual, I went to the glove compartment and grabbed mine. I took the safety off and chambered a bullet.

"Asta," I called out as soon as I hit the door. I didn't give two fucks about alarming anybody that I was there I wanted the muthafucka to know I was there and try some shit so I would have a reason to body his ass. "Asta where you at it's me Ky?" I yelled out again.

The room to the back door opened, and I guess that was

Simon standing there looking like a raging bull. He was guarding the door like I wouldn't move his dumb ass.

"Where the fuck is Asta?" Zan asked already losing patience. That was normal for him though he never had any patience for anything.

"She ain't here, and you're trespassing so if you don't want to go to jail I suggest you get the hell out of my house." He said with more bass in his voice than I cared to hear.

"The fuck is Asta nigga, and that's my last time asking," I said taking in his appearance. His clothes were disheveled, he had scratches on his arms and face, and there was blood on the white shirt that he had on. That shit threw up some red fucking flags. I walked towards him, and he stood back like he was ready to fight. I put the safety back on my gun and placed it in my back.

"I'm not gonna ask you again get the HELL—" I cut that nigga off with a right to the jaw. It knocked him off guard for a minute, but he regained his balance and threw a jab at me and got me on the shoulder. I fucked him up with a two piece, and his ass hit the floor. I stepped over him, as bad as I wanted to fuck him up I needed to check on Asta first. As soon as I turned that corner, I saw her limp body laying on the ground.

"Oh fuck Asta baby wake up," I yelled as I kneeled down beside her. I put her head in my lap. I checked to see if she was breathing and she was, and then I checked for a pulse, and there was one, and I was relieved. Anger slowly crept up through my soul looking at the bruise on her neck from where he had choked her. "Zan call the fucking ambulance man," I yelled out, Zan was too busy stomping the fuck out of that nigga. “Zan,” I yelled, and he snapped out of it and stepped in the room to call for help.

“Oh, my Godddddddd!” I heard Neala squeal coming into the room. “Whaat did you do to my sister.” She started kicking Simon as he was trying to get up. She started raining blows on him; her little ass was quick as shit with them hands too. Once he got his footing, he pushed her down and took off towards the front of the house. Zan threw the phone down and ran after him. All you could hear next were gunshots and then tires screeching.

“Oh shit Asta,” I said when I heard her take in a deep breath. “Shit ma you scared me.” I hugged her, and she winced in pain. I let her go and touched her side, and she broke down crying. “What happened ma?” I was so mad, my first instinct was to run after that nigga but Asta needed me, so I let Zan handle that.

“That muthafucka gone, I shot him in the muthafucking ass though. I bet that nigga won't be able to sit right for a month.” Zan said walking over to Neala who was standing over Asta and me. “You good?” he asked Neala and then looked at me. “She good?”

“I don’t know man I need to get her to a doctor.”

“Oh shit,” he said and picked up his phone remembering that he was supposed to be calling for help, he shook his head. “Fuck it let's just go; we can get her there faster.” He grabbed Neala by the hand, and they walked out. I scooped Asta up bridal style and carried her to my car and put her in the front seat. Zan jumped in with Neala, and we headed to the nearest hospital which happened to be Presbyterian Main.

The minute I got Asta situated and comfortable I was going

on a hunt for that nigga. He was gone pay for this. I hated a muthafucka that thought it was okay to put his hands on a woman. I was gone show him why that wasn't such a good idea, and the fact that she was my woman was even worse. I was gone make sure that he paid for every bruise and every ounce of pain he caused her and I put that on my life.

SIMON

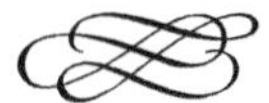

I tried to hold in the tears that were threatening to come out but I couldn't, the pain that I was feeling was like no other. I had never been shot before, so when the bullet tore through my ass, I didn't know what to think. I just knew there was a crazy gang banger chasing me and I had to get away. Thank God, I left my keys in my car. I was headed in the direction of the nearest hospital.

I don't know how I was gonna explain this to my father. The first thing he was gonna want to do is call the police, and I couldn't do that. If I called the police, then I would be arrested for what I had done to Asta, and that would not be good for my career.

My vision was starting to get really blurry, and I couldn't keep my eyes open. I knew it was a bad idea trying to drive after I had gotten shot, but I didn't have a choice. It was get in the car or be killed. I tried to pull the car over, but I lost control and hit a tree head-on.

~

A constant beeping noise woke me up, I tried to open my eyes, but they were so heavy. I took in a deep breath, and the smell of ammonia caused me to panic a little. I tried my best to remember what happened, the last thing I remember was trying to get to the hospital. I tried to jump up because I remembered that I had gotten shot, but I was hooked to cords.

"Calm down son." The voice of my father instantly put my mind at ease.

"Where am I?" I asked still looking around confused.

"You're in the hospital." He said, and then it registered, the smell of ammonia and the bright lights and cords. This was the fanciest hospital room that I had ever seen but knowing my father, he paid extra to have things like this for me.

"What the hell happened and how did you get shot." His tone was filled with anger, but it was even. He was trying to stay calm, but he was eager to get answers so the culprit could pay for what they had done to me.

"I don't know dad, just let it go. I was in the wrong place at the wrong time." I tried to convince him that it was nothing but I knew he wasn't going to go for that. My only issue is that if I tell him what happened I would also have to tell him what I did to Asta and that was a conversation that I wasn't ready for. Not because I put my hands on her because my dad was my instructor in that department, but because he told me to get her out of my life a long time ago and I didn't listen.

"Simon, you will tell me who did this, and they will pay for it." His voice raised a few octaves. He was no longer trying to keep his cool he was about to blow, and I knew it.

"Dad I—"

"I will not keep having this conversation with you. When you're ready to tell me what happened, I will listen, but until then I don't have anything else to say." He stood up, and I knew that if I didn't say something he was going to start snooping and finding shit on his own and that was the last thing I needed.

"You can't press charges."

"What! Why the hell not?" he yelled completely forgetting where we were.

"Because, I almost killed Asta and me getting shot was retaliation from that." He sat back down and attempted to digest what I had just said. He didn't quite know how to respond, so he just sat quietly and waited on me to continue. "She went to some biker thing with some guy named Ky, so I confronted her about it, we argued, and I told her that you were right that she wasn't worth my time and in the heat of the moment, she let me know that she slept with the guy. I lost it, dad. I don't know what came over me I just lost it." I laid my head back on the pillow and thought back to everything that happened. "I didn't even hear anyone come in the house. I don't even know how they knew to come there; she didn't call anyone, I made sure of that."

We sat there in silence for what felt like forever I didn't know what to think. I knew he was mad because he just kept shaking his head. He always said that Asta would be my downfall, but I loved her, and I couldn't help it. Looks like he would be getting his wish though.

"How many times have I told you that girl was no good for you?"

"I know dad but—"

"No buts, hopefully now you've learned your lesson. Stay the hell away from her." he pointed at me to let me know that he wasn't kidding. "I'm gonna have someone go to the house and remove her things and deliver them to her sister. Then I'm selling the house because it's not safe." He threw out demand after demand, and for about 20 minutes I sat there and listened to him tell me what he was going to do and what I was going to do. After a while, it started going in one ear and out of the other. "Did you hear me son?" he yelled once he realized that I wasn't paying attention.

"Yeah dad I—"

"Oh, my God Simon what else does this little hood rat have to do for you to see that she means you no good." He shook his head, and I just looked at him. It didn't matter what I said about the matter it wouldn't help, and I knew it. "Hannah is a nice, beautiful woman who loves you to death and not to mention she looks good on your arm. What are you gonna do with that DJ huh? What she gone come play some of that hippity hop shit at one of our functions? I think not; this is for the best son. Move on with Hannah, and y'all can raise this baby together."

I knew that bitch was gonna go behind my back and do some shit like this. I told her that I didn't want kids right now and I damn sure didn't want any with her. I care for Hannah, and I was definitely satisfied with her in the bedroom, but it stopped there for me. I didn't see a future with her; I was gone keep her around long enough to make Asta act right then she was gone. Too bad I wouldn't get the chance to do that now.

"Oh my God baby are you alright?" my mother walked in and rushed to my bed.

"Linda he's fine, stop making such a big fuss." My dad barked. I could feel my mother tense up when she heard him raise his voice; she should be used to it because it was nothing new. He talked to her like that often. I used to question if he loved her with the way he treated and talked to her but I guess that's just his way. He had been like that for as long as I could remember. I had grown to accept it, and she had too.

"He's my only child Charles; you can't expect for me not to worry."

"Who do you think you're talking to Linda?"

"Charles, I—" before she could finish her sentence he got up and slap the shit out of her. She grabbed her face and walked around him and sat down in the chair beside the one he was sitting in. Sometimes I felt bad for my mother because she was a sweet woman and she took damn good care of me, but hey she chose to stay so I guess she was okay.

"I'm sorry to interrupt." I heard Hannah say; I didn't even realize that she had come in the room.

"Oh no need to say sorry Hannah, please please come in." My dad stood and grabbed her hand and escorted her to the seat that he was sitting in beside my mother. His lustful stare and the sneaky grin on his face made me question the real reason he was pushing for me to be with Hannah so bad and from the look on my mother's face she was thinking the same thing.

"Are you okay Simon." She asked in her sweet voice. I could see the light bruise on her neck from me choking her before I left the office.

"Yeah, I'm okay."

"No, he's not, he got shot in the ass by some hoodlum." My father turned his attention back to me. "I'm hoping he learned his lesson and you two can start to build something nice together, I'm so excited about my grandbaby."

"What!" my mother squealed. She looked back and forth between the three of us waiting for an answer. "Simon?" she questioned, and I shrugged and turned my head. I reached up and hit the morphine push button, so I could take my ass to sleep.

"I just found out that I was pregnant." Hannah beamed.

"When were you going to tell me, son?"

"Leave the boy alone, he's grown and if he wants to start a family, he can." My dad threw daggers with his eyes at my mom, and she sunk into her seat and glared at me. I wasn't in the mood to talk about this, and I wasn't going to.

"Y'all can leave now, I'm tired, and I just push some more medicine, so I'll be sleeping soon." I looked at all three of them in the face, and they all stayed put. I shook my head, closed my eyes and let the morphine take me to a happy place.

ASTA

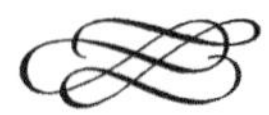

"I can't believe this muthafucka," I said looking at the bruises on my neck that were slowly starting to fade away.

Ky was itching to get his hands on Simon, and I knew that it was only a matter of time before he ran into him. He told me that he had found out where Simon worked from Wolf but thank God Simon wasn't there when he popped up. I knew that Simon's dad had a lot of connections and the last thing I wanted to do is to have Ky in some shit behind this. He already fucked him up, and Zan shot him in the ass so to me that was enough. I mean I'm alive, and I would just make him pay with seeing me succeed without his punk ass.

I sighed deeply and walked out of the bathroom and into the room that I was now staying in at my sister's house. Her spare room was nice as hell and very spacious, being comfortable wasn't an issue. Neala was happy that I was staying with her and I was trying to get used to it.

Ky tried to get me to come and stay with him, but I couldn't do that, we didn't know each other well enough to live together, and I promised myself that I would never be dependent on another man for as long as I live. The next house that I move into, my name will be on the deed.

"Sisssstttterrrr," Neala yelled out from the living room.

"What?"

"You've got company." She sang.

I hopped out of bed and headed to the living room. As soon as I turned the corner, there stood Ky in some stonewashed Levi's and a black polo with some red and black 11's. I couldn't stop the smile from spreading across my face. It didn't take much for the butterflies to start swarming in my stomach. I loved the feeling that this man gave me, even though I was trying to force myself to take shit slow I couldn't help but get excited when I saw him.

"Go get dressed

"Bitch don't be cheesing now." Neala rolled her eyes. "You been in that damn room all day and his black ass pop up and you standing there drooling."

"Why I gotta be a black ass," Ky smirked.

"Cause yo ass two shades lighter than coal bruh." She got up and walked down the hall to her room and shut the door.

"The fuck wrong with your sister man?" Ky laughed

"Cause she been trying to get me out of this room all day and I just ain't felt like it." I shrugged.

"Why the hell not?" He walked up on me. I swear I didn't think he knew what personal space was.

"I just ain't been in the mood."

"I can take care of that for you." He looked me in the eye, and I knew exactly what he was talking about.

"So where are we going and how should I dress?" I attempted to change the subject. Catching on to what I was doing he laughed.

"Match my fly," he shrugged and took off towards my room. I just shook my head and followed him. There was no need in me objecting because his ass wouldn't have listened anyway.

When I walked in the room, he was sprawled out on the bed like he lived there, had even kicked his shoes off. I just stood there watching him. For a while he ignored me then he raised his head, "keep staring at me like that, and you can forget this little date, I'ma bend yo ass over and give you what you want." He licked his lips and laid back down. I knew he was serious so I went to the closet and found me something to wear.

As bad as I wanted to feel everything he could offer I wanted to go out just as much. I needed to get out of this house and who better to do that with than Ky. I would never say that to my sister though, she would have a damn fit.

I settled on a black jumper that tapered at the ankle and paired it with this bad ass pair of red bottoms my sister got me for my birthday this past year. I hadn't even gotten to break these babies in.

I heard light snoring coming from Ky, so I slipped off into the bathroom to get showered and dressed. Turning on the water to the right temperature and jumping in. I stepped into the running water and stood there letting the water run down my body as I reflected on all the shit I had been through in the last couple of months.

I went from being in a dead-end relationship with Simon to finding a man that woke up every dead emotional cell that I had in my body. I hadn't known Ky long, but I knew I didn't want to be without him. I hated that he was mixed up in the shit with Simon and me, and if I could help it, I would keep him from getting into anything else.

"Why he still calling and texting you Asta." I jumped because I was so lost in my thoughts that I didn't know that he was even in the room with me.

"Who?" I asked genuinely confused.

"Don't play dumb with me Asta." His voice was low, but I could hear the anger in it. "So this nigga putting his hands on you and you still talking to him."

"Who Simon? I don't talk to his ass. He's called and text but if you look, not once did I answer or text back." I don't know why I felt the need to explain myself, but I did. I didn't want him to think that I was still having conversations with Simon at all. Then it hit me, "Wait why in the hell you going through my phone."

"Because I can."

"What if I go through your phone?" I said and turned off the water and slid the curtain back.

"I—you—it—fuck it" he got to where I was in less than a damn second. Our lips collided as he gently lifted my wet body out of the tub. “Damn’ he mumbled against my lips. I could hear him unbuckling his pants. I attempted to stop him, but he knocked my hands away.

“Wait I thought we were—”

“Shut up.” He demanded and then sat down on the toilet with the seat down and pulled me over there with him. He grabbed his dick and nodded for me to sit down on it, I bit my lip and obliged. I straddled his lap and grabbed his dick and placed it at my opening and slid down on it exhaling on the way down. “Fuck girl.” He grunted once I made it to the base.

I had to sit there for a second to relish in the moment because I was on the verge of an orgasm already. Once I got my bearings, I started moving in a slow back and forth motion. I threw my head back because he was taking me to another world. The way he filled me up made every little move he or I made intense.

Grabbing the back of my head, he pulled me to him, and our tongues wrestled. He snatched the ponytail holder that held my long ass dreads off and grabbed a handful and jerked me back and covered my breast with his mouth.

“Mmmmm” I moaned, but when he bit down on my nipple, I felt my orgasm rise. “Shit I’m about to cum.”

“Ummhmmm.” He moaned as he continued to work on my breast.

“Oh fuck, sweet Jesus,” I called out, and he scooped my legs up in his arms and bench pressed my little ass. “Shit baby.” I moaned as he slammed me down on his dick.

“Got damn baby.” He called out, and he lifted me up and down his length. “I’m bout to nut shit.” He bit his bottom lip, and

I held on for dear life as he took me for the ride of a lifetime. "Shit shit shit!" He moaned out and threw his head back and bit his lip.

"Oh, Ky." I cried.

He lifted me up a few more times before he lowered me slowly onto his lap and moved his arms from under my thighs. He grabbed me and pulled me into his chest and hugged me. I wrapped my hands around his neck and hugged him back.

"What the fuck you doing to me girl." He said into my neck.

"The same thing you doing to me." I kissed the side of his face.

"Good so we on the same page." He leaned back and looked at me in the eye. "We seeing where this goes right?" I just looked at him, I mean I just got out a relationship. As if he was reading my mind, "I know you just got done fucking with that bitch ass nigga, but this is right, it feels right." The sincerity dripped from every word he said, and it made me believe him.

"Just be patient with me."

"Just be honest with me." I nodded. "So, when in the hell were you going to tell me that bitch was still fucking contacting you. The pussy is banging but not enough to make me forget." He smirked.

"I ignore him, there was nothing to tell. He just keeps apologizing, and I don't want to hear it. I wish he would just leave me alone."

"Call him."

"No Ky, it will just make things worse."

"Nah, I'm bout to make that shit stop! Call him or I will. I got his number out of your phone, so the choice is yours. If you call him I will behave, if I have to do it then shit gone get real."

"You don't trust me to handle it?"

"That ain't got shit to do with it Asta, just forget it, I got it." He nodded and lifted me off of him and turned the shower back on. He finished taking off the rest of his clothes and hopped in. After about a minute or so he looked out the side of the shower curtain. "You coming, we got shit to do."

I rolled my eyes and hopped in the shower so we could get ready for whatever it was he had planned. I had a feeling that he wasn't going to let the Simon thing go until he was satisfied that he got the punishment he deserved. I just hoped he didn't get into trouble in the process.

KY

Asta thought she was slick, she was trying at all cost to keep me away from that bitch ass Simon but what she failed to realize was that I had resources and if she wouldn't tell me then I would find out my damn self. If I had to do all the work, I was damn sure gone have a lot of fun when I got to him. I tried to get her to understand that, but she blew it off so Simon could thank her for the ass whooping he was about to wear.

"Ohhh yay I love Chima's." Asta squealed as we pulled up. Chima's was a Brazilian restaurant where they walked around with meat on the stick and carved you fresh meat at your table. They would keep bringing you that shit until you turned that little card over that let them know that you were done. A nigga eats so much in here, my ass be leaving with meat sweats.

"Yeah, I know." I glanced at her, still not feeling the fact that

Simon been calling and texting and she didn't tell me. We hadn't known each other long, but we had built something that I thought was strong enough for her to tell me that the man that assaulted her was harassing her. I was trying to be there for her, and in order for me to do that, I needed for her to be honest with me.

Once we got in the restaurant, we ordered our drinks, and for a while, we just sat there in an uncomfortable silence. Every now and then she would look up at me, and I would just stare at her until she broke it and went back to her phone. I was about to break the ice when her phone rang. She looked at it and then back up at me, I was about to grab it until she answered it.

"This is Asta." I calmed down because I knew she wouldn't answer the phone for him like that, not while I was sitting here. "Absolutely." She beamed and then touched her throat, and that pissed me off. "This Monday?" she questioned the called and whatever they said made her smile so big I had to join in. "Thank you so much, and I will see you then." She ended the call, and I patiently waited for her to tell me the good news. "I got the job at 92.7." she was still smiling.

"Damn A, that's what's up. I'm happy for you." I got up and pulled her out of her seat and hugged her. I didn't give a damn that we were in a crowded restaurant, I knew that she had been working hard as hell to get here and she finally had.

"Thank you." She kissed my cheek. "For everything."

"What I do?" I let her go and walked back around to where I was sitting.

"Just being you, you put in a word to help me get this job." I was about to interject, but she stopped me. "Wolf already told me."

"Wolf talk too got damn much, I didn't do that shit for no other reason than to help you get to where you've been trying to go." I put that out there I didn't want her to think that I did that just to get with her.

"I know that you've been nothing but genuine with me since the day I met you at the mall. I swear in the short time I've known you, you have been more to me than Simon ever has and we were together for years."

"Well, that's the difference between him and me."

"I'm so glad I looked past that ugly ass fisherman hat that day at the mall." She giggled.

"Wasn't shit wrong with my hat, I'ma wear that hat tonight while I'm making you scream." I bit my bottom lip to let her know that I was serious.

"Damn Ky," she crossed her arms over her chest and then looked around the restaurant to make sure that no one heard what I said because I damn sure wasn't quiet. "Seriously though, thank you for being there for me through all this bullshit and showing me that not all men are the same."

"Hell, no cause they don't make em like me no more."

"Conceited ass."

"Nope." I reached under the table and ran my hand up her leg. "I just know what I'm capable of." She jumped, I laughed and then sat back in my seat.

She got quiet and then looked at me in the eyes, "I don't want you to think that I'm trying to protect Simon because I'm not. I just don't want you to get into any trouble behind this mess. I mean I feel like he got punishment enough, you kicked his ass and Zan shot him in the ass." She shook her head. "Just leave it alone, I want to move on," she paused. "I want to move on with you."

"You didn't have a choice with that A, even though we haven't known each other that long you have managed to fuck with a nigga's emotions and I don't let that happen." I patted my heart. "I ain't saying I love you or no shit like that because I still got a lot to learn about you but a nigga care for your beautiful ass." She blushed. "I wanna see where this can go." She nodded. "But I'm telling you right now, I ain't letting this shit go with Simon until I put hands on him. My daddy always said that a man that will hit a woman needs to be shown by a man how that shit feels."

"It's not—"

"It really doesn't matter what you say A, it's gone happen and sooner rather than later." I shrugged, and she sat back in her seat and just looked at me. I couldn't really read her expression.

"Just be careful, I don't do good with jail visits." She giggled.

"Oh, you wouldn't hold a nigga down Asta?"

"Umm I didn't say that, but I won't sit here and say that I'm bout that life either. Just being real."

"Ah shit, I can't do shit with you if you ain't no ride or die." I got up like I was about to leave and the look on her face was priceless.

"Are you fucking serious?"

I laughed and sat back down. "No baby girl, I knew that when I met you and that's why you're here." I winked at her, and the first wave of meat came though, we talked and laughed while we stuffed ourselves.

I don't know what it was about Asta, but she brought out a whole other side of me. I was sitting here spilling my guts about my ex and how much I cared for her. I told her how she left me and how I turned to other women to cope. Like I was having a whole live Dr. Phil moment going on but the shit felt right, so I didn't give a fuck. Asta listened, and she understood where I was coming from. I knew about her relationship because we had talked about that shit before but she told me how she didn't get along with his parents and shit like that.

"Oh no." she said and threw her napkin on the table.

"What's up?" I was confused because we were having such a good time.

"That's Simon's father." She rolled her eyes. "Charles Washington in the flesh."

"That black ass muthafucka is Simon daddy?" She nodded. "His mama must be made of fucking paste then." She laughed as I got up and headed in his direction.

"Ky no, please."

"I ain't gone do shit, I'm just going to introduce myself." I walked away before she could say anything else.

I wanted to smack the smug look that was on that muthafucka's face as I was walking up. He must have known who I was because he excused the flunkies that were at the table with him.

They looked at me with confused looks as they walked passed me to the front of the restaurant. When I got to the table, we just stood there and looked at each other for a minute before the pompous asshole opened his mouth to speak.

"You don't think I know who you are." He waited on me to respond, but I didn't, I kept my facial expression neutral. "You're nothing but a thug, Ky'sier J. Brasher 27, son of Kender and Michele Brasher. Rides motorcycles for a living when he's not slinging dope." He whispered the last part like I gave a fuck. "You're noone and if it wasn't for my son and that little no good bitch sitting over there you would be in jail." He growled.

I smiled, "Charles M. Washington 58, son of Margret and Charles Nkrumah. What muthafucka, that last name was too black for you?" I grabbed a chair and turned it around backward and sat right in front of him. "Shouldn't be seeing as though it looks like God himself painted yo black ass with charcoal." I got serious. "Just like you can find shit out so can I, just like I'm gone find out where yo bitch ass son is. I will sit outside of ya business, ya house, and as soon as I find where the white bitch stays, I'm gone sit there too until I get my hands on that pussy you raised. You teach him that it was okay to put his hands on women? Huh bitch?"

"You think I'm scared of you; you're nothing but a thug." His voice was shaky and didn't match the words that were coming out of his mouth. "You are going to stay away from my son or—"

"Or what?" I stood up. "The longer it takes for me to find his bitch ass the more pissed I'm gone be and then I'm gone take that shit out on you." I put the chair back where it was. "And before you start wracking your brain about if that was a threat, it was." he didn't say anything else, and I said what I needed to, so I walked away and joined Asta.

Her eyes were on me the entire time that I walked back to the table, they were filled with worry. I walked straight to her and kissed her long and hard. I wanted her to feel safe and secure with me. For as long as I was breathing she wouldn't have to worry about shit.

"What did you say?"

"Nothing you have to worry about."

"He looks pissed."

"He should be." I laughed. We paid the check and headed out of the restaurant. As soon as I opened the door and walked out, I heard someone call my name.

"Ky'sier!" I stopped in my tracks because that voice was one that I was sure that I never thought I would hear again. "Oh my God it's so good to see you," Lovey said as she walked up and hugged me like Asta wasn't there. I didn't play that disrespectful thing, so I cut the hug short and lightly pushed her from me. She leaned back and looked at Asta, "Oh, I'm sorry. I'm Lovey, Ky's ex-girlfriend." She extended her hand for Asta to shake and instead of taking it Asta just nodded her head and smiled.

"I'm gonna go ahead to the car Ky." She said sweetly, and I leaned down and kissed her and told her I would be there in one minute. Once she was gone, I turned my attention back to Lovey.

"What's up Lovey?"

"Damn Ky that's all the love I get?" she tried to hug me again, and I took a step back. The way she just up and left me still fucked with me every now and then so her popping up acting like shit was all good wasn't cool.

"Don't sit here and act like we good, what you did was fucked up Lovey and you know it. The only reason I stopped is because I didn't want to be rude and I didn't want my girl to think I was hiding shit."

"Your girl?" she questioned, and I nodded. "Ky she's not even your type." She laughed.

"What's my type? You?"

"Well yeah." She ran her hand down the length of her body.

It was my turn to laugh. "She's nothing like you, and honestly that's the first thing that attracted me to her."

"Don't act like you don't miss me Ky."

I just looked at her because I wasn't going to admit to shit. True enough I missed Lovey, I loved her and I wanted to build a life with her but she wasn't loyal, and that was important to me. Asta was slowly taking over any ounce of feelings that I may have had for Lovey.

"We need to get together and catch up Ky."

"Nah can't do that."

"Just as friends, I'll respect your little girlfriend." She smirked. "Well, at least I'll try." She reached into her purse and pulled out a card and handed it to me. I looked down at it, and against my better judgment, I put the card in my pocket.

Without another word, I walked back to the car and got in, surprisingly Asta wasn't upset. She didn't ask any questions, and she didn't want to hear anything about what we talked about even when I tried to tell her. She said that, that had nothing to do with her and she was good. I smiled, and we went back to my house to finish our night off right.

RONDO

This baby shit was fucking up my life something serious. Char was not talking to my ass at all, and it was starting to piss my ass off, but I knew I had to give her time. She didn't deserve any of this, and I had to do what I needed to do to make it right, starting off with going to pay Rachel a fucking visit.

From the minute I saw her walk in that hotel with Ryan I knew that I was going to have to have a conversation with her whether I wanted to or not. Heading the direction of where she lived I sat back and thought about shit, I fucked up, like really fucked up. I just needed to make sure that Rachel didn't make shit any worse for me. I prayed like hell that it wasn't my baby, hell I only fucked once. From the looks of it, Ryan hits that on the regular so maybe his soldiers got there before mine.

I had yet to see Ryan; I needed to let him know that his services were no longer needed within the Carolina Kings. I knew this shit wasn't his fault, but he could've come at me better than that. What he did was reckless, and it pissed me the hell off, and I didn't need people like that around me.

Pulling up to Rachel's I noticed that Ryan's car was there, I could kill two birds with one stone. Getting out of the car, I could hear yelling coming from the house.

"How in the hell you didn't know that we were affiliated?" he yelled.

"Because I wasn't in yo shit like that, you didn't tell me anything about you or what you do."

"But you knew who Rondo was though."

"Who doesn't know who he is Ryan, had I known you knew each other I would have gone about shit a different way." she yelled.

"What you would have told my ass that I was a possibility and not the father, had me walking around looking like a fucking fool. Tell people this my baby, and you don't even fucking know."

"This is your baby, Ryan."

"Bitch don't fucking play me," he growled, and then I heard her scream, and I walked in the door and pushed him away from her. Even though she was a scandalous bitch, she was still pregnant.

"Nigga you gone killed the bitch, she pregnant my nigga," I said to Ryan who was looking like he wanted to take my fucking head off.

"What the fuck do you care? Life would be better for you if the bitch was dead right."

"That's a bitch move, and I don't shake like that."

"Thank you," Rachel interjected looking back and forth between the two of us.

"Had yo hoe ass not have been trying to be scandalous then none of this shit would have been happening." I narrowed my eyes at her.

"Well if you wouldn't have been out here cheating on yo bitch you wouldn't have to worry about any of this shit."

I couldn't even say shit, as bad as I wanted to cuss her ass out, I couldn't because she was right. Had I been thinking straight I wouldn't have ever cheated on Char, and I wouldn't be sitting here trying to reason with the woman that may be carrying my seed.

"Look I just came here to say stay the fuck away from me and my girl, when the baby born call me and I will come up and get a test done, other than that we ain't got shit to talk about."

"So you ain't trying to support me through this pregnancy."

"You a dumb ass bitch." Ryan yelled and shook his head. His ass was pacing back and forth in front of her couch. I was watching his ass because if he made one wrong move it was gone be lights out for his ass.

"Hell no, I didn't want this and I don't even know if this baby is mine, his, or somebody fucking else's to be honest. I don't put shit past you."

"I'm out of here, I don't got time for this shit." Ryan said as he pushed past me.

"Aye, first if you ever touch me again it's gone be some hymn singing and flower bringing feel me, second stay the fuck away from my shop." He just glared at me and if I wasn't mistaking I could have sworn I saw him smirk. I had a feeling he was gone be a got damn problem.

"Rondo, I don't want to go through this shit alone." She whined.

"Do it look like I give a fuck about what you want? Just stay the fuck away from me and mine."

"And if I don't."

"Then all my morals go out the window and they gone find you ass floating down the Catawba River." I threatened and then left her standing there with her mouth hanging open. I wasn't fucking playing with her. Until that DNA test comes back and lets me know that I need to have communication with her, I plan to act like the bitch don't exist.

~

"Welcome to Char Styles." The receptionist greeted as I walked in the door. I nodded at her, and she smiled and went back to doing whatever Char paid her ass to do.

Looking around, it made me feel like shit. Here this woman was beautiful, smart and making a way for herself and doing a damn good job of it, and I'm out here about to fuck up a lose her. That made my heart ache.

“Char, can I talk to you for a minute?” I asked as I walked back to her station.

“Not right now Rondo.” She said without even looking up at me. She was almost done with the client she had so she was about to talk to me whether she wanted to or not.

“Now or I can sit in that chair and stare at your beautiful ass until you do.”

“Awwwweeeee,” the girls in the shop said in unison and that pissed Char off.

Char was a private person, so I knew that they knew nothing about what was going on with us. She was not the person to air out her dirty laundry. So the fact that they thought I walked on water when it came to our relationship aggravated her because she knew the truth. Right now, I was a fuck up, and I could admit it.

I watched as she finished the last curl in the client’s head and then she tucked, combed and ran her hands through the girl’s head until she had it just the way she liked it.

“What do you think?” She smiled.

“Char you are the shit, and you know it.” the client ran her hands through her hair. “Thank you, girl, how much?” they handled business, and I decided to go to the office and wait for her to finish.

Pictures of us decorated her wall in her office. I walked around and looked at the various pictures we had taken during our ten plus years. I heard the door open, but I didn’t turn around to address her, I walked over to the first picture that we had ever taken.

"Our first date, you remember that?" I wasn't expecting her to answer I just wanted her to listen. "I knew right then that I wanted to be with you for the rest of my life." I sighed. "I kick myself every_day for not marrying you sooner."

"Why so we could be going through a divorce right now?"

I turned around quick as hell. "Baby listen, I fucked up, and I'm sorry, I'm so fucking sorry. The shit happened once, that's it. You got to believe me." she didn't say anything, but I could see the tears forming in her eyes. "Please baby you can't leave me, we can get through this," I begged.

"A baby." Was all she said.

"I'm sorry."

"Sorry can't fix that Ron."

"I know, but I will do whatever you need me to do."

"Right now, I just need space."

"No, I can't do that."

"Ron, you don't have a choice."

"We weren't even together Char, you left me."

"For one got damn day! God forbid it had been more, who knows how many chaps would be walking around here calling you daddy."

"You know it's not like that."

"I don't know shit Rondo, after ten years." She looked around the room. "I don't know shit. I may have been mad, and I might have left and said that it was over but did you really think that I would give all of this up." She moved her hand around the room at all of the pictures. "for an argument?"

"I didn't know what you would do."

"So, you go out and fuck a bitch raw after being broken up for less than 12 hours?

"Char I wasn't thinking straight."

"No Rondo you did exactly what the fuck you wanted to do, you wanted to go and fuck a random bitch, and you did now look." She yelled.

"Why would I do that when I have you. If I have you I don't need anything else, Char."

"Except the one thing I can't give you." A fresh set of tears flowed down her face, and I reached out to console her, and she backed away. "I really need to get back to work."

I looked her in the eyes, and I wanted to shed a few tears myself. I felt like I was losing her slowly but surely. The one thing that I would never be able to do is to watch her be happy with some one else. Fucked up part about this whole situation is that I actually get to feel what Noble felt all those years ago, shit was ironic, but unlike him, I was gone make sure she didn't go anywhere.

I walked up on her quickly and kissed her on the cheek, "No matter what I want you to know that I love you with everything in me. Please don't ever forget that."

Heading out of the shop, I bumped into a familiar face. I wondered if Ky knows that Lovey was back in town. She didn't even bother to speak to me, and I was okay with that, I didn't care for her ass anyway. I pulled out my phone and ordered Char her favorite bundle from Edible Arrangements and had them send it right away. I also ordered her a bouquet of Calla Lilies which was her favorite flower. Gifts weren't gonna get me back in her good graces, but I was gone send them until she told me to stop, even then I wouldn't stop until she agreed to sit down and talk about us. Drastic times called for drastic measures, and I was not about to live without my woman.

RYAN

I wanted to shoot the shit out of Rondo but I knew if I did I would no doubt have to worry about Ky and Zan coming after my ass and I didn't have the time or the man power to deal with them. Ky and Zan made a name for themselves when they were in the game, and I wasn't trying to bring their asses out of retirement.

Rachel's ass better be glad that Rondo came in when he did because I had every intention on choking the life out of that bitch. Then she gone have the nerve to ask him was he gone support her through the pregnancy, what the fuck she mean?

She told me that there was no other possibility of anyone else being the father of that baby, but I should have known she was lying. I mean got damn I fucked her on the first night and from the sounds of it so did Rondo. I guess the fact that she made me embrace the whole fatherhood thing, I overlooked certain facts.

When she first told me about the baby, I told her that I wasn't ready and she made me believe that I was the greatest thing in the world and I believed her so I started to get excited and now it has been snatched away from me.

Then on top of all of that Rondo tells me that I no longer have a job, like any of this shit was my fault. I was an innocent bystander in all the bullshit, why the fuck was he upset with me. She played me just as much as she played him. I needed to talk to Noble because I needed money and now he was the only person that I would be able to get that from.

"My friend," Noble answered on the first ring like he was anticipating my call.

"We need to talk business man."

"I was thinking the same thing, come through." He disconnected the call.

I knew I was getting in business with the devil but Rondo left me no other choice, I was so close to having all the money I needed for my restaurant, I had to do what I had to do. I just hoped no police was involved; I just wanted to keep doing what the fuck I had been doing. I had a friend or two still in with the Kings, and they would tell me the schedules so I could plan the pick ups around that. My phone rang, and it was Rachel, for some reason I wanted to hear what she had to say.

"What!" my tone was nasty, and I wanted her to know that shit wasn't cool by a long shot.

"Ryan I'm sorry, don't do this, I don't want to go through this alone." She whined, and I laughed.

"You must really think I'm dumb as hell, he says fuck you,

and you come whining to me. Do I have fool written across my forehead Rachel?"

"No Ryan, I—"

"You what? Think I'm a got damn idiot, nah fuck you call when it's time for the DNA."

"So you just gone abandon me at a time like this?"

"You can't be serious right now, you lied about me even being the father, you just fucking played my ass in front of Rondo. Fuck you bitch." I ended the call because she was making me want to turn this fucking car around and go finish what I started. She really think I'm a fool, I may not be the finest nigga around but I aint' desperate.

Pushing all that shit out of my mind I pulled up to Noble's warehouse that was on the outskirts of Charlotte. I parked around back like normal and hopped out, I headed in. When I walked in I stopped in my tracks because there were a few uniforms standing in there talking to Noble.

"Aye my man." He waved for me to come in but I didn't move. I didn't fuck around with the police. "It's cool, they." She pointed back and forth between the two cops. "Are cool."

I made my way and just stood there while they talked about what Noble needed for them to do concerning Rondo. There had to be more to the story with him and Rondo if he was doing all of this shit. Rondo said some shit about him wanting Char when all that shit came out but that couldn't be it either, I was damn sure gone ask his ass when the officers left.

"So how in the hell are the drugs gone get in the building?" the one officer asked.

Noble nodded at me, “That’s what my man right here is for, he works for them.”

“Use to work for them.” I corrected him.

“Small details, you’ll figure it out.” he shrugged.

“Okay well just let me know when the drugs are in there and we will be there.”

“My man.” Noble dapped them up and saw them out. I didn’t know how to feel about all of this, but at this point, I really didn’t have a choice because I needed the money.

Noble walked back in and waved me to his office in the back. He sat down in the chair behind the desk and motioned for me to have a seat. I shut the door then sat down in front of him. Before he could say anything, I got straight to it.

“Look Rondo fucked me, and I got shit to do feel me.” he just nodded so I continued. “But before I get into all of this I need to know what the fuck is going on and why.”

“You don’t need to know shit.”

“If I’m putting my life and freedom on the line I need to know more than you think.” I looked at him, and he looked at me and then he sighed.

“Fine, what the fuck you wanna know?”

“What the fuck is this about.” He looked at me.

“Now that is none of your business.”

“Well, I’m out.”

“Only way out is death.” He threatened, but I knew he needed me at this point, so I stood up and prepared to leave.”

“Well you just gone have to kill my ass then because I’m not about to do all of this shit not knowing what the fuck I’m doing it for." I opened the door and started to walk out before he spoke.

"Rondo is my half-brother." I stopped in my tracks and looked at him to make sure I heard him right. "Muthafucka you heard me, that nigga my brother and he don't even know it."

"So if he don't know what's the fucking problem."

"Cause that nigga been fucking with me ever since he was fucking born. When our dad got my moms pregnant, he told her not to call him for shit, that he didn't want shit to do with her or me. That fucked moms up, she was prideful so she didn't ask him for shit and she tried to raise me on her own. That shit got to be too much, so she turned to drugs and alcohol."

"What does this have to do with Rondo?"

"If you shut the fuck I'll tell you muthafucka." He barked, and I returned to the seat that I was sitting in before I attempted to leave. "Me and Rondo grew up together not knowing that we were brothers, but he always thought that he was better than me. In school, sports, and in the streets." The mug on his face showed his true disdain for Rondo. "Then shit topped the cake when he got with Char after she left my ass. That made me hate him, I should have killed his ass, but HIS father threatened my life when he found out I was planning to do just that and take over his shit, so I backed off. Now I'on give a fuck, I was a little fucking kid back then let him try that shit now."

"So this is over Char and your daddy not loving you nigga?" I asked confused.

"No this is about showing that nigga what pain feels like," he snarled, "Pain like I've felt."

I chose not to ask anything else because this nigga was foaming at the mouth, he was so pissed. I let the subject go, and we talked about the shit he had planned and how much it was gone pay. Money was the motive for me, so I needed to make that clear.

CHAR

No one knew the pain that I was going through right now. To know that you can't give your man the one thing that he wants and then find out that he went and got it with someone else. I loved Rondo more than I cared to admit and starting a family with him meant more to me than anything, just thinking of the fact that it may never happen hurts my heart.

The night after Ryan blew up his spot he begged me not to leave him, he swore it was just one time and that it would never happen again. Before that night I hung onto every word that Rondo said to me but now the trust was gone, and I didn't believe shit he said.

After all of that, I hated myself for still loving him, I couldn't make myself leave him. I'm not a dumb bitch by far, but this man has been my everything for the last ten years. I wasn't letting his ass off that easy though, for the last few weeks he been sleeping in the guest room. Putting in work was an understatement, he was cooking and cleaning, bringing home gifts and flowers, I mean he did that shit before, but now he was extra with it.

"Morning beautiful." He opened our bedroom door with a tray of food.

"Hey." I just couldn't shake the fact that he may have fathered a child with someone else, so I wasn't with all the pleasantries. I respected the effort that he was trying to put it but that's about as far as it went.

"How you feeling this morning?"

"Good!"

"Got damn it, Char, will you stop that shit." he threw the plate down on the bed spilling the orange juice and further pissing me off.

"Exactly what the fuck do you want me to do Rondo." If looks could kill his ass would be a dead muthafucka.

"I want you to stop this." He waved his hands around. "If you gone forgive a nigga then do that but I ain't trying to be around here walking on egg shells."

"Are you fucking kidding me?" I asked incredulously. "Please tell me what the fuck you would like me to do Rondo, just forget the shit and hop back on ya dick? Got damn!" I yelled. He gets like this from time to time, he wanted me to let all this go, and we go back to being the "perfect couple," and that was not gonna happen. "You broke my trust not the other way around and some burnt ass toast and a dozen roses ain't gone fix that shit!" I pushed the plate off the bed, and it hit the floor.

I didn't know exactly what he wanted from me, if I could just forget it all and move on that easily, I would, but every time I think about him giving her what was supposed to belong to me I get sick to my stomach. Hell, I was doing good just being here.

"I just want us to try and work this out Char, that's all I'm saying."

"No, you want me to forget and that shit ain't happening."

"I want you to have a conversation with me with out the little smart ass one-word answers." He went back to raising his voice, and when he did that, I tuned him out. He was mad at the wrong person, he should be mad at himself.

"I can't be who you want me to be right now Rondo, you hurt me." I could hear the tremble in my voice, and I was silently cussing myself because I made a promise not to cry over this shit anymore. I have given him enough tears.

"Char don't cry." He rushed over to try and console me, and I pushed him away, and he sucked his teeth. "See this is what I'm talking about, I'm trying to be there for you and you pushing me away.

"Where the hell were you when you were dicking ol'girl down and making babies and shit. Huh? You didn't give a fuck then now did you?"

"Char you left me, you told me it was over. You packed yo shit and left. Technically I didn't even cheat so what the fuck?"

"So we break up for one night, and you thought it was okay to go out and fuck somebody, I mean damn you moving on that quick? If that was the case, you should have left my ass where I was. You came looking for me the next day, so you can save that bullshit." I screamed at him.

"I FUCKED UP okay Char I fucked up, is that what you want to hear. My heart left when you walked out that door and told me that you were done with me. I didn't know if it was out of anger or some final shit! I had never heard you talk like that Char, we don't do that so when you said it I thought you were done." He put his head down.

"SO WHY DID YOU COME AFTER ME? If you knew you fucked that bitch why follow me all the way to my sister's house? Why not just leave me where I was and continue to do you?"

"Because I love you Char and you know that." He looked at me, and I shook my head I was tired of arguing about this.

"I need time Rondo, this some heavy shit."

"You don't think I know that Char, you don't think this shit tears me up every time I look at you or hear you crying? I know the shit wasn't right and I'm sorry. I just want us to make this work Char. I'll do whatever you need me to do, to make this work."

"Do you still talk to her?" I looked him straight in the eyes so I could make sure that he wouldn't lie to me.

"Not now, no."

"What does that mean?"

"I haven't seen or talked to her since right after Farmington."

"What about before?" he took a deep breath like he was about to prepare himself for something.

"I saw her a few times before, Farmington. I had to, so she wouldn't tell you." He dropped his head.

"So you was still fucking her." I smacked my lips and hopped up off the bed he was about to catch these hands, and he knew it because he ran over and grabbed my arms.

"Hell no, I didn't lie to you when I told you that I only fucked her one time. And like I said I was drunk out of my mind."

"No excuse."

"I wasn't making one Char, listen." He turned me towards him as I was trying to get away from him. "I fucked her because I was hurting, that's the only reason. When she told me she was pregnant I freaked out, she said as long as I was there for her and the baby she would keep her mouth shut and I needed her to do that until I found out if the baby was mine or not." He took a deep breath. "I felt like shit the moment I was done with her, it was the worst mistake I ever made, and I put it on our unborn kids that it will never happen again." He put his left hand on his heart and his right in the air.

I sat down on the bed and lowered my head in my hands. I broke down, he came and comforted me and for the first time since it all went down I let him. How in the hell was I supposed to accept a child in my life that was the result of his infidelity? I didn't give a shit what he said, just because I yelled out some shit while I was mad didn't mean that we weren't together and he knew that no matter how he tried to spin it.

"I don't know if I will be able to accept the baby," I said with my head still in my hands.

"Huh?"

I looked up at him, "I don't know if I will be able to accept that baby." I made sure he heard me that time. I could tell what I said to him hurt him, but I had to be honest with him. I knew that put him in a situation because who would want to be with someone that didn't accept your kids? I would leave him before I ever made him choose.

"I need you, Char." He put his head in my lap. "I love you." He was getting choked up and that caused me to get choked up too. "I don't even know if the baby is mine, I fucked her one time. It may be Ryan's baby." He pleaded. "Please baby just ride this out with me."

"Rondo, I love you more than you will ever know but I love me too." we hugged and cried for a while before we both went our separate ways with the same amount of answers that we came here with.

ZAN

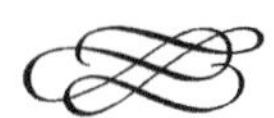

"Fuck!" I yelled as this sexy ass red bone that I had just met in the strip club finished sucking me off in the bathroom. Bitch was thirsty as hell to chill with me, and I told her that she could if she sucked my dick and next thing I knew she was in the bathroom doing her thing.

"So I'm chilling with you tonight right?" she asked as she wiped the nut off her face.

"Um yeah whatever," I shrugged. She could bring her ass in the VIP if she wanted but that's as far as things would go with us. I had no plans on having any dealing with her after we left this bathroom. After I washed my hands, I left out of the bathroom and ran into Ky. When he saw the red bone come out behind me, he shook his head and laughed. "What shit, I ain't had no pussy in two fucking days."

"To each its own my nigga," Ky dapped me up and headed to the bathroom.

I walked to the VIP section, and ol' girl followed me. I guess the gentlemen thing to do would be to ask her for her name, but I didn't care to know it, so I said fuck it. I plopped down in the chair in front of the stage, and red bone attempted to sit in my lap. I stopped her ass before she could get comfortable.

"The fuck you doing?" I asked her with my face scrunched up.

"I thought we were chilling?" she asked with a pout on her pretty face.

"Yeah, we are, I sit here, you sit there, and we chill, got it?" I pointed to my seat and then to a seat across the section, hoping that she would get the hint. That head job only granted her the entrance to the VIP not to the Zan experience. I hated when bitches got that shit confused. She rolled her eyes and headed to the table where the drinks were, fixed her a drink and came right back and took a seat in the chair right behind me. I wasn't trying to deal with this shit tonight.

I was already ducking Tash's ass I was not about to add another crazy bitch to the equation. My phone vibrated, and I looked at it and speaking of the got damn devil, she was texting me threatening me once again. I shook my head and focused on the stripper that was shaking her ass all in my face. I could hear ol' girl behind me sucking her teeth, so I turned around and looked at her.

"You need a tooth pick or some shit?"

"What?"

"You back here sucking yo teeth like you got some shit in your teeth, you good?" I yelled over the music, and she nodded her head and continued to sip her drink.

"ZANDER!" I heard my name being screamed from across the room.

"Man got damn!" I yelled and threw my self against the chair. "A nigga can't come out and see some ass in peace." I was loud enough to get the strippers attention which caused her to crawl over to where I was and started putting on a show. She was showing out and had my full attention, so much that I forgot that Tash had just walked in the building. That was until she grabbed the stripper by her hair and drug her off the stage. "The fuck Tash." I tried to break up the fight, but she was dogging the hell out of that stripper. "Break that shit up,"

I finally got a hold of Tash and threw her off of the stripper. The stripper was trying her best to get to Tash to redeem herself.

"Yo sweetheart she just whooped yo ass you would think that you would be grateful that someone pulled her off of you." I lightly pushed the stripper back. "But if you wanna keep acting like you bad and shit I can definitely let her ass go."

The stripper took heed to my warning. Security came over to make sure that shit was okay when they saw it was me they laughed and went on about their business. They knew me here, so they knew that I had whatever this was under control.

"And who are you?" the red bone said putting herself into Tasha's sight.

"Bitch who the fuck are you and why are you speaking?"

"I'm Lira, and we're chilling tonight," she said pointing back and forth between the two of us. I threw my head back because I knew she had just started a whole new issue.

"Nigga I can't leave you alone for one got damn second without some shit popping off" I heard Ky bitch ass say as he was walking in the VIP section.

"Shut the fuck up Ky, that's Tash dumb ass up in here acting fucking stupid."

"No, I'm sick of you disrespecting me Zan."

"Oh my God I don't know how many times we got to go through this shit, how in the hell am I disrespecting you if we ain't together. I'm starting to think yo ass is retarded or some shit." I shook my head. I just didn't understand where she got that we were anything other than parents to Z2 and fuck partners when I wanted it. "You are my b-a-b-y-m-a-m-a nothing more nothing less."

"Hello!" the Lira bitch sang.

"What!" Me and Tasha yelled at the same time.

"Look Lira, is it?" I questioned, and she smacked her lips like she was offended that I didn't know her name acting like she didn't just suck my dick in the bathroom of a strip club. "Honey I don't know what you thought was gone come out of this but ah you ain't got a chance in hell with me. You don't even know how to suck dick without using your teeth so I know good and damn well you would never be added to the team."

She was about to say something, but my phone alerted me that I had a text so I looked down and I saw that it was Neala, so I threw my hand up to stop her. I read the text and smiled. I was about to get rid of Tasha's aggravating ass and head to see my baby.

"You are so rude." Lira snapped me out of my thoughts of getting in between Neala's legs as soon as I got to the house because the picture she just sent me of her in the nightie definitely had my dick on swole.

"Yeah, I know that shit, now if you would excuse me, I got somewhere to be."

"Nigga, I came with you." Ky jumped in.

"Well bring your ass."

"I'm going with you, we need to talk." Tash turned like she was about to follow me.

"The fuck if you are, listen and listen good. I don't want you to miss anything that I'm about to say." I got right in her face. "WE ARE NOT TOGETHER! Stop trying to act like we something we ain't, I fuck you, yes, but that's as far as it goes. Chill the fuck out and just wait for your turn, I'll call you next week."

With that I walked off and headed to the exit, I didn't have time for her shit, and I hoped what I said sunk in. Tash was convenient pussy and good pussy. I didn't want a relationship with her, I didn't want anything with her, but God saw fit for us to share a child.

"Zan" I heard right as we were exiting the club. "Ky'sier why haven't I heard from you?"

"Ah hell naw." I threw my hands up and looked at Ky, there was no way that she was back and from the looks of it Ky knew. "You knew she was back in town?" he nodded his head. "Nigga, Asta!"

"I got this nigga, what's up Lovey. I ain't had time." he simply said.

"Well I would really like to catch up with you, I've gotten settled in my place and my new job now I want to have some fun."

"Well go in there and rub on some titties cause Ky ain't allowed to have fun, we got shit to do." I pushed past her, I hated her ass, and I knew that she was no good for Ky, but that nigga loved that bitch.

"You ain't changed a bit." She said looking at me.

"Neither have you, still the same ol' gold digging, uppity ass bi—"

"Bruh let's be out." Ky cut me off, and I mugged his dumb ass I wanted to rock his ass because he was already taking up for the bitch. The fuck. "I'll holla at cha Lovey."

"No the fuck he won't."

Ky pushed me out of the club, "Nigga you wild."

"Don't you even think about it." I pointed at his gullible ass.

"You ain't even got to worry about that, I'm on my way to see Asta now." He smiled, and I nodded.

"Shit I'm headed that way too." We hopped in the car and headed in the direction of Neala's house.

NEALA

I looked down at my phone and saw that Pink had texted me for the thousandth time today. I rolled my eyes in my head and grabbed my phone to text him back. Before I could hit send, he was calling.

"Why you ain't text me back?"

"You didn't give me a chance to text you back Pink."

"I wanted to know what you were getting into tonight."

"Tonight, I'm chillin, I'll holla at you tomorrow." I sighed.

"You must be with that bitch ass nigga tonight." I had to move the phone away from my mouth so he wouldn't hear me laugh. Pink knew that Zan was the furthest thing from a bitch especially since he played his ass not once but twice. "Hello"

"I'm here, no Pink it's just Asta and me tonight."

"Well let me come over, your sister don't care."

"Nah not tonight."

He was starting to get on my nerves, after that day in the front of my house I fell back from Pink because every time we would talk he would bring up Zan and I didn't have time for that shit. I just started back accepting his calls a week ago, and he's starting this bullshit again.

"You use me to entertain your ass when that nigga ain't free. You only call when it's convenient for you." He huffed. "I don't even know why I still fuck with you. I thought you gave a fuck about a nigga."

"Here we go with this shit, this is why I don't fuck with you Pink. You knew what it was from the beginning, so I'm unsure as to why you crying about the shit now."

"Okay look, let me just come over so we can talk."

"You know what, bye Pink."

I hung up the phone, and it rang with a text from Zan telling me that he and Ky were on the way. Since that night in Farmington, me and Zan had been getting really close. So close that the shit was starting to scare me, which was why I was still dealing with Pink's aggravating ass.

"He's still calling you." Asta laughed.

"Girl"

"You just need to cut his ass off, he gone fuck around and hurt you for playing with his feelings like that."

"He will fuck around and get hurt fucking with me."

"Aight billy bad ass." We heard the door open, and Asta looked at me, I guess she just now realized that Zan had a key. "Why in the hell does his ass gotta key."

"Cause he took the spare that I was gonna give you out of the basket and never gave that shit back."

"Why in the hell are you worried about it?" Zan pushed past Asta, and she pushed him in the back.

"You better keep your hands off my woman," Ky said walking up behind Asta.

"Yo shut the fuck up nigga, didn't even have a niggas back tonight." Zan shook his head and collapsed on the bed.

I was too scared to ask what happened that he would need Ky to have his back, there was no telling what the fuck went on. He stayed in some shit with his baby mama and I guarantee that's exactly what it had to do with. Before I could ask anything, I heard banging on the door. I looked at Asta, and she shrugged her shoulders, and I looked at Zan, and he stood up.

"That better not be Black bitch ass."

My heart started beating when I saw Zan take the gun out of his waistband. Pink was the kind of person that didn't take no for an answer which is why he always came back around when I blew him off. I would hope that he wouldn't just pop-up over here especially after his last run-in with Zan.

Zan took off towards the door, and I followed closely behind until I felt myself being pushed back by Ky who also had his gun out. They looked at each other then opened the door with their guns trained on the unwelcomed visitor. When the door swung open, my blood began to boil.

"What the fuck you doing here Tash," Zan asked putting his gun back in his waistband.

"Man, here we go with this shit, if y'all fuck up my night I'm going the fuck off on the both of you." Ky pointed at Zan and his baby mama.

"Why the fuck are you here, and who's house is this." She fussed, and Zan was trying to block her from seeing who was inside, but I wasn't for all that, so I made sure to let my presence be known. "You with this bitch." Tasha tried to rush her way in, and Zan stopped her.

"Let her ass go," I stated calmly.

"Nah ain't no need for all that, Tasha dumb ass shouldn't have followed me any got damn way. What the fuck did you not understand about the shit I said at the fucking club huh?"

I don't know why but a part of me got pissed knowing that he was with her right before he came here to be with me. I knew we were just chilling and it wasn't anything serious but that shit still got under my skin. I wanted to take his head off and hers. I needed to fall back from his ass and fast. I was starting to feel shit for him, and I wasn't about to be dealing with this shit because he couldn't stay the fuck away from her.

"I don't care what the fuck you talking about Zander, as long as we got Z2 and you still fucking me, I got the right to do as I please. Now let me get to this little nappy headed whore."

"Let her go," I said with a little more bass in my voice. I was starting to get mad. She was now disrespecting me by coming to my house, and I wasn't built for it today.

"You heard the bitch let me go." She taunted.

"Man go the fuck on with the bullshit, you ain't about to fuck this up for me."

"Fuck what up Zan, what like I fucked yo night up with the

little bitch you said sucked yo dick." She laughed, and I laughed too and decided to join in on her childish antics.

"Hell, that bitch just got the party started for me, you know that first nut always comes fast." I shrugged. "Looks like it's gone be a good night for me."

I guess that got under her skin, but she rushed past Zan and got her hands on my shirt. I snatched away from her and grabbed her by the little bit of hair that she did have. She swung and caught me on the side of the face.

"Uhnhhh." I hear my sister say.

I got a good hold of her hair and just started jabbing her in the face. She was swinging all wild, but I couldn't feel that shit for nothing, my adrenaline was at an all-time high and I was mad as hell. She tripped over something and hit the ground, I jumped on top of her and continued to rearrange her fucking face. Zan grabbed me and tried to pull me off, and when he did that, somehow she was able to sneak one on me and popped me in the mouth. I jumped up and swung and hit Zan in the mouth.

"Don't you ever grab me." I was mad as hell that she was able to sneak that shit in. I turned around right as she got on her feet. Mad was an understatement, and I was about to show her just how much. We started going toe to toe, and I was wearing her ass out. I hit her one good time, and she hit the floor. I grabbed her by her bald ass head and drug her out the door. My hands kept slipping through that shit, the more it did the madder I got. When I got her outside of my house, I kicked her in the stomach.

"Bitch don't you ever bring your ass back to my got damn

house. You think I fucked you up this time; you don't want to know what I can do with my Louisville slugger in there." I threatened her while she coughed uncontrollably. I turned around and walked back towards the house. Zan was standing there mugging me. "Yo ass can get the fuck out and go with her." I walked past him bumping his shoulder as I passed.

"You better calm yo little ass down, I ain't going no got damn where." He yelled out as I walked to the back of my house.

"Sis you good."

"Yeah babe, I'm mad as fuck that bitch hit me in the mouth, but I'm good." I tucked my bottom lip, and I tasted blood, had me wanting to go back out there and beat her ass again. "I'm going to bed, make sure he gets the fuck out of my house."

I walked into my room and locked the door. I didn't want shit to do with him. I couldn't deal with all his shit with that crazy ass bitch. I was not about to be fighting her every other day, nah that was not about to be my life. I cared about Zan, and the sex was amazing but the way my attitude set up, I ain't trying to go to jail.

I could hear him shaking the doorknob, I looked at it and walked into the bathroom to wash my face and check out my lip. I looked, and it wasn't swollen yet, but I knew it would be soon.

"Neala open the door man." He sounded aggravated and tired, but I didn't give a fuck. I was mad as hell, and that trumped whatever he felt at the moment. I didn't bother to respond I took off my robe that now had blood on it and threw it in the trash, hopped in the bed and turned off the light. I thought that Zan was gone because I didn't hear him say anything. "I'm going to the fridge to grab a beer if you don't open this shit by the time I get back I'm kicking the fucking door knob off."

Turning over and ignoring his ass, I closed my eyes and tried to forget about the bullshit tonight. I thought that we were gonna have a damn good night tonight. I bought this bomb ass nightie, I had plans on pulling some tricks out the bag for his ass, and he had to go and fuck it all up.

Once I finally got comfortable, I heard him turn the knob again before I could get my laugh out good I could hear him kick the door knob twice and the damn thing came falling off. I sat up and looked at his ass through the darkness. He didn't even bother to say anything just walked to the side of the bed that he normally slept on, took his clothes off and hopped in. Didn't apologize or nothing. I snatched the covers and rolled over. I couldn't stand his fucking ass.

The next morning.

"What the fuck," I said as I slowly opened my eyes to see Zan's dick in my face. "What the hell do you think you doing."

"You owe me for putting yo hands on me, and I want my payment in head." he looked down at me and I pushed him back.

"You got to be out of your got damn mind if you think I'm putting my mouth anywhere on that thing and you were with your baby mama last night and some other bitch. My ass ain't walking around here on fire." I sat up in the bed and stretched. I looked down because something felt weird. That's when I noticed that my nightie was hanging off my arms I pulled on it. "Did you cut my fucking nightie?"

"Hell, yeah I did, you wasn't trying to let me see you in it, so I cut that muthafucka."

"You owe me eighty fucking dollars."

"I'on owe you shit!" he stood there naked jacking off while he was arguing with me. I couldn't help but look because the man had the prettiest dick I had ever seen but right now wasn't the time to think about that. "Stop looking at my dick."

"Get out of my house, and you won't have to worry about me looking at ya dick."

"I ain't going nowhere but between yo legs as soon as we get this conversation out of the way."

"Ain't shit to talk about, that was way too much. I am not about to be fucking ya baby mama up every time I see the raggedy bitch, and that's what a happen because that bitch is mad disrespectful."

"I got her you ain't got to worry about that anymore."

"You said that the last time and the bitch ended up on my doorstep." I shook my head. "As long as you fucking with her, she ain't never gone fall back, and I don't want to deal with that shit Zan."

"Aight well she cut the fuck off."

"Don't do that shit because of me."

"What the fuck Neala, you want me to stop fucking with her or not. I'm confused as hell right now and horny as fuck." He said still jacking his dick.

"Could you stop that." I snarled up.

"No, now next topic of discussion." He said looking right at me. "The other bitch I met at the club, and she sucked my dick in the bathroom. That was it, I didn't even know that hoes name."

"And you think that shit okay?"

"Yeah"

"Man, just get out."

"Nope," he shook his head. "We just chilling, we said if shit gets serious on either of our ends we would talk about that shit. So, is there something you want to tell me?"

I didn't answer him because I didn't know how to. I didn't know if I was ready to open up myself to another man the way I did with Rodney. Especially with a man like Zan. Being around him was fun but was that enough to build with? Zan would hurt me, and I knew it.

"Nope." Was all I said.

"Well shut up and take this dick."

Before I could say anything, he was in bed between my legs slowly sliding into me. We both gasped and enjoyed the euphoric ride that we were on. After today I was gonna distance myself from Zan as much as I could, it was the best thing for the both of us.

CHAR

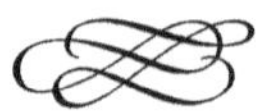

I could hear the sound of the engine coming down the street, I took a deep breath because no matter how much I tried to separate myself from Rondo he always made his way to where I was. I couldn't even have a damn cigarette in peace. The minute I saw the gold-plated bike come into my sight my guard immediately went up and my attitude made its way to the forefront.

"Why you gotta look so mean Char?" Rondo asked as he took his helmet off and placed it on the back of his bike. No matter how mad I was at him, I couldn't deny that I was still madly in love with him. What I would give to just be able to go back to what we were just months ago.

"I'm tired and I got a lot of shit to do today."

"Will you go on a date with me tonight?"

"Ron—"

"Damn it, Char, I'm trying. I don't know what else you want me to do. I want to make shit right but you gotta niggas hands tied."

"Fine Rondo, we can go out." I threw my hands up.

"Wow, it's like that?"

I looked at him like he had lost his damn mind, "What the fuck do you want from me, Rondo? You can't tell me that I don't have the right to be upset."

"You got every right to be upset but got damn I said I was sorry, the shit happened one night that we were broke up." He kept throwing that shit out there like it made a damn difference. He knew that we were not broke up his ass just wanted a reason to go and fuck a bitch.

"I'm sorry don't explain no got damn baby and you lying about the shit."

"I didn't lie."

"Muthafucka, omitting the truth is lying no matter how you twist it." I pointed at him. I could feel the tears trying to form, and I shook them off. I was tired of crying, even though the shit was killing me I was not about to let him see that shit anymore.

"Aight, Aight, I lied, and I was wrong. I should have told you."

"Yeah, you should have."

"Can we get past this? I need to know if I'm wasting my time or not."

"You ain't giving me time to get over it; you think I'm just supposed to say oh well it was an accident everything is good." I threw my hands up. "It's not that simple Ron, you out here making whole babies."

"We don't know that, that might not even be my baby."

"That's not the point Rondo."

"Well what's the point!" he raised his voice. I noticed that one of my stylist had just pulled up and I didn't want that hoe to know my business. Bailey was nosey as fuck and if she knew your business then everyone in Charlotte, NC knew your got damn business.

"Can we talk about this later," I said a little sweeter because Baily was walking by. Rondo chuckled.

"Yeah." Was all he said before he hopped back on his bike and burnt out. I just sat there watching as he left.

I didn't understand why he felt that I didn't have the right to be upset about all of this. I know I had been hard on his ass, and I wasn't trying to hear too much of what he was trying to say right now, but I was still in my feelings. Maybe it was time to sit down and talk about all of this so that we could see where we were gonna go from here.

My biggest fear is that this baby is his because I don't know if that is something that I would be able to deal with. Everyday I would have to look into the face of an innocent little baby and be reminded of my man's infidelity. I don't even wanna get started on the baby mama drama. I had way too much to lose to even think about that shit.

I took out another cigarette and lit it up, seeing as though I wasn't going to be trying to have a baby no time soon, so I picked back up my bad habit. Halfway into my cancer stick, I noticed an all-black Toyota Camry coming down the street at a slow pace. I didn't know the car, and then I remembered I had a new client coming in today. Thinking that it was her, I took a few more tokes of my cig and bent down to put it out when I looked up my mood instantly went sour.

"Char, right?"

"You know exactly who I am, let's not be cute." I gave her all the attitude I could muster up at the moment.

"Whoa, why we got beef. You shouldn't be mad at anyone but your man." She said rubbing her belly.

"You right Rachel I have no issues with you, so I'm baffled as to why you are here in from of my establishment." My hands found their way to my hips out of habit.

"Okay look, this started off all wrong. I just came here to have a conversation—"

"About?" I cut her off, and she sighed and took a step back.

"Look, I just wanted to first apologize for my part in any pain all this may have caused you. He told me he had a girlfriend after—"

"Fiancé!" I blurted out.

"Right, fiancé."

"So, you knew about me?"

"Yeah after we had sex the one time he told me that it was a mistake and that he and his girlfriend had a fight and things got out of hand and that he was going to make shit right with you."

"SO, then my issue is with you too. Its women like you out here fucking our men and—"

"Your man was a willing participant, and I didn't find out about you until after the deed was done, but I didn't come here to argue with you. I just wanted to see if you could talk to Rondo about his decision to support me through this pregnancy."

"Bitch you done lost your everlasting mind, hell he doesn't even know if the baby is his. Didn't you just say y'all only fucked the one time?" I snarled my nose.

"All it takes is one time and—" I cut her off again.

"And how many times did you fuck Ryan for him to think it's his baby." I gave her a questioning look, and she just sat there for a second. She opened her mouth to say something but then closed it again. "I thought so, IF the baby is Rondo's, then HE will move accordingly."

"WE gone have to deal with each other at some point." She pointed back and forth between the two of us.

"Yeah, the jury is still out on that." I crossed my arms across my chest.

"Hey Char," I turned to see Asta and Neala walking down the side walk. The mug on Neala's face was cute. "What's going on?"

"Oh, Rachel here was just leaving."

"So we can't finish this conversation?"

"There is nothing more to discuss."

"I think there is." Rachel put her hands on her hips standing her ground. I was about to cuss her out, but Neala interjected.

"Look bitch, yo face ain't pregnant, so I suggest you keep it moving before you piss me off. I done already had to handle one dumb ass baby mama who don't know her place, I won't mind making it two."

For a minute Rachel stood there looking back and forth between the three of us. I was now laughing because Neala ass didn't have it all. Rachel scoffed and then headed back to her car and pulled out. I turned to look at the girls, and we all shared a laughed. I pulled out another cigarette and Asta snatched and threw it.

"That shit is nasty and you too pretty for that."

I looked at her, and for the first time in a while, I just broke down crying. I had started bottling up my feelings about the whole situation and pouring my everything into my work so I wouldn't have to think about it. I was hurt and borderline depressed; I just wanted all of this to go away, I wanted my life back.

"I need a girl's night," I said wiping my face. That's the one thing that I was starting to love about these girls. They were there for me with no judgments, they didn't try and fix me they just let me cry and wiped my tears while listening to what I needed to say. I had never had real friends like that, and I was glad that Ky and Zan had placed them in my life even though I hated them right now.

"Well, let's do this," Neala said smiling.

"What the hell happened to your lip?" I asked her and Asta laughed.

"Girl let me tell you." She started, and we sat outside the shop while she told me the whole story about her infamous run-in with Tasha, the baby mama from hell. I had a much-needed laugh, and we planned our girl's night, and I was looking forward to hanging out and getting drunk, not having to think about anything or anyone. But before I do that I was gone be sure to tell Rondo about his bitch coming to my shop!

KY

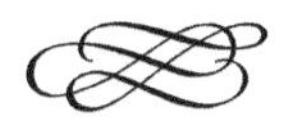

Anyone who knows me knows that I'm not a very patient person, and the fact that this muthafucka got me riding around town looking for his ass is pissing me the fuck off. I know his bitch ass daddy told him what the fuck I said too. I was not gone be satisfied until I got my hands on his bitch ass.

"Nigga how long you plan on sitting here, you know we got shit to do," Zan said snapping me out of my thoughts.

"I'm bout to pull out his bitch ass still hiding and shit. Been over a got damn month and he still MIA." I shook my head and went to crank my car.

"Today yo lucky day my nigga." Zan tapped me on the arm and then nodded towards Simon and the white bitch headed in the building where he worked. I smiled and grabbed the handle to the door and got out. "Yo nigga leave yo gun in here, I ain't trying to go to jail."

I looked at him and thought long and hard about that. I knew what I was going to do and if shit got hot, the last thing I needed was to be caught with a got damn gun. My ass was a felon, and I knew that was automatically a sentence. I put my piece in the dash and Zan threw his under the seat.

I could feel my adrenaline rushing as I walked in the building like I owned that muthafucka. As soon as we walked in, the reception lady greeted us with a huge smile. She was a small ass Asian chick and from the way she was staring us down she lived for black meat.

"How can I help you, gentlemen." She smiled and focused her attention on Zan. She looked him up and down and then licked her lips.

"You can forget that shorty you can't do shit for me but cook a nigga some rice." Her eyes got real big, and I shook my head. "Nigga you saw that, licking her lips and shit."

"Excuse me, sir, I'm sorry but—"

"Look at her damn mouth I can't even fit my dick in there." he continued.

"Where Simon Washington's office at?" I asked trying to change the subject.

"Do you have an appointment?" she looked at her computer and then back up at me. She was trying her best not to look in Zan's direction.

"Her ass don't speak fucking English either." Zan started typing something on his phone. "Where is Simon Washington's office." And I looked at him and then laughed when his phone repeated what he said back in what I'm guessing was Chinese.

She just glared at him like she was offended, as funny as the shit was I didn't have time for it.

"You are very rude." She said

"That's what they tell me," Zan said walking off after me.

"You can't go in there; you don't have an appointment." Completely ignoring anything she had to say I headed into a set of double doors that led to the offices in the back. I walked down the hall until I came up on the door that read Simon Washington. When I walked in that muthafucka looked like he had seen a got damn ghost.

"What's up bitch."

"Get out of my office, you're trespassing."

"Didn't you try that shit last time and where did that get you," I said and bit my bottom lip as I headed over there and started raining blows on his face. He was trying his best to fight back, but I was on a mission to rearrange his face, so he didn't have a fucking chance. "So you like to beat women huh?" I yelled at him as he lost his footing and fell. I walked around the desk and started to stomp his ass out. I was so mad I blanked out, and I didn't come too until I felt someone grab me.

"Nigga it's me, you gone kill that muthafucka." I heard Zan say and my body relaxed.

"The muthafucka deserves to fucking die." I yelled.

"What the hell is going on in here." I heard Simon's punk ass daddy say. Just hearing his voice pissed me off I turned around and headed in his direction. "Hannah call security."

"Bitch you move and Ima choke the shit out of you." Zan threatened and she stood there not knowing what to do.

"I told you that the longer that muthafucka hid the more pissed I was gone be and I was gone take that shit out on you." I got close enough to rock the shit out his black ass. "Next time yo black ass a listen, I stepped over him because his ass was out like a light. When I got to the door I turned back around. "Don't fucking contact Asta again, if I have to come back yo bitch ass won't be walking up out of here." I threatened and me and Zan walked out.

"Ky what are you doing here?" Lovey walked up to me.

"The fuck are you doing here?"

"I work here, what's going on why are you bleeding?" she started looking me over.

"Ky lets go man we ain't got time for this shit." Zan said as Lovey walked passed us and looked in Simon office.

"Oh my God Simon." She said and turned to look at me. "What in the hell is going on?"

I didn't even bother to answer but I would definitely be hitting her up later on to see what the deal was with that. Zan made sure to blow kisses at the receptionist on the way out the door. I shook my head and made my way to the car.

~

"It's ya girl DJ Sass coming through on the one's and two's." I could hear Asta doing her thing from the hallway and I was so proud of her. This is what she had been waiting for, I'm glad I could help her reach her dream.

"Hey what you doing here, I still got promo to do so I'm not off just yet."

"Oh I know I just wanted to see your face, damn A, can a nigga just wanna see his woman?" I joked with her.

"I like the sound of that."

"Good, I'm all about kidnapping and shit." I lowkey threatened her.

"You're crazy but—" something caught her eye and she started looking at my hands and then my face and finally she landed on my boots. I should have changed clothes before I got here but I didn't, I wanted to let her know what was going on before anyone else could. Just in case Simon's bitch ass didn't listen and contacted her anyway. "What happened? Are you okay."

"Oh that nigga fine." Zan said walking around the corner. "It's them other niggas." He stuffed a handful of chips in his mouth.

"What is he talking about?"

"I paid ya little boyfriend a visit, if he contacts you again you better let me know"

"What did you do Ky?"

"I beat his ass and then I knocked his bitch ass daddy out." I smirked and Zan laughed.

"I asked you to leave it alone."

"And I told yo ass that I wasn't going to so."

"What if they call the cops?"

"My homeboy one of the best got damn lawyers around and I got money." I shrugged. "Then I'm fucking them both up again."

She lowered her head and I started to get pissed. I didn't know if she was mad about me fucking them up or if she was mad because she still care about that muthafucka. I took a step back and looked her in the face.

"What's this really about?"

"Ky don't do that."

"Nah you don't do that. Do we have a problem?"

"No baby, I just want it all to be over." I sucked my teeth and took a few more steps back.

"Oh aight." I shook my head and turned to walk away. She didn't even bother to call after me and that pissed me off even more. I grabbed my phone and shot Lovey a text telling her that we needed to talk. I was mad and that probably wasn't the best idea but oh fucking well.

LOVEY

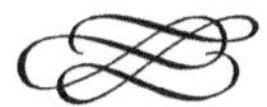

"How do you know him?" Mr. Washington barked as he headed over to help Simon off the floor.

"We used to date a long time ago." I didn't know if me answering that was a good idea, when all he did was nod his head I figured everything was okay so I walked back to my office to check my emails and messages. When I saw a message from Ky saying that we needed to talk it was bittersweet, bitter because I knew I had to answer to why I up and left all those years ago and sweet because just seeing his sexy ass brought back so many memories.

I met Ky when he was in the streets, he was a big deal around our way and I lived for that life, the thrill of it excited me. The money, the cars, and the shopping sprees it was everything I ever wanted. Then all of a sudden, he got a conscience and wanted to leave the game. I begged him to stay but he wanted to ride that fucking bike.

Everything became that bike, no matter how much I complained or bitched at him he didn't care. It had gotten to the point where he was gone damn near every weekend at some race and when he wasn't he was in the shop working on his bike. Money was still coming in but it was nothing like the money he made from the streets and what he did make most of it he poured into the bike.

I tried one last time to get him to see things my way and when he told me that this was life for us I knew that he wasn't the man for me. And when I found out I was pregnant I had to get the hell out of dodge because I knew Ky and I wasn't trying to be struggling with a baby. Hell, I wasn't even ready for a baby. I waited until he went away for a weekend and I left, took all of my stuff and some of his. I cleaned the safe in the house and moved in with my mother up in Hickory, NC.

Ky called me for months until I finally got to the point where I couldn't take it anymore, so I got a new phone and number. I loved Ky, I did, but I loved his status and money more so without that there was nothing for me, not even with his child inside of me. My mother found out I was pregnant and forced me to keep the baby, our family didn't believe in abortions. The plan was for her to take the baby once she was born, but the baby ended up being still born.

Oddly enough that shit hurt more than I could ever imagine, I didn't think that I wanted to be a mother, but the more time past the more I was starting to enjoy the idea of motherhood and then it was all snatched away from me.

It took me a while to get over that, and the fact that I had to go through all of that alone put me in a horrible place. Now I'm better and I was working on getting my life straight. I went to school to get my real estate license and landed the job of a life time here in Charlotte at Washington Realty. It seemed like this was all fate that my job landed me here and I run into Ky not once but twice. Maybe we were meant to be.

"Hello" I sang when Ky answered the phone.

"What's good." His tone was cold and uninterested but I knew better, he missed me I could see it in his eyes that night outside of the restaurant.

"What do we need to talk about?"

"When did you start working there?"

"The better question is what were you doing up here showing yo ass?"

"He put his hands on my girl." Him mentioning his girl put a bad taste in my mouth. He hadn't been serious with anyone since I left, I knew that because Tasha, Zan's baby mama and I were cousins and she kept me up to date with everything. We weren't close or anything like that but she came through when I needed info.

"Umph," I grunted.

"You know what this was a mistake."

"No, no Ky I'm sorry, I just—it's just—"

"Just what Lovey? You don't want to go there with me."

I could still hear the hurt in his voice even though he would never admit to it. He wasn't feeling the way I left, and I didn't blame him, but he knew my position, and he chose to ignore it. What was I supposed to do, I would have resented him, and we would have been miserable so me leaving was best for the both of us.

"I guess I got some explaining to do."

"Nah not really, you don't owe me shit."

"But I want to."

"If this is some kind of—"

"It ain't nothing like that," I lied because the minute I saw his chocolate self I knew that I wanted that old thing back. Just thinking back to the way he used to take his time with my body, boy did that man know his way around the bedroom. "Can we have dinner and—"

"I don't think that's a good idea Lovey."

"It's just dinner, not like we gone sleep together or anything." Not that I didn't want to, I would work my way into that, but right now I would just settle for a dinner date. "Just have dinner with me for old times sake."

He hesitated but eventually, he agreed, I couldn't contain the happiness I felt. I was on my way to getting my man back. I didn't care what he did as long as his ass was raking in the dough and according to Tasha, he was doing just that. I ended the call with Ky and sat back in my chair, I couldn't wait until Saturday night. My thoughts of Ky were interrupted by Simon, my boss's son.

"Lovey we need to talk."

NOBLE

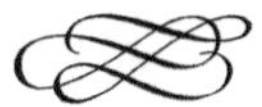

I sat across the street from Char's shop, I just knew that the woman was meant for me. I was just young and dumb back then. I didn't know what I had until I saw her on the arm of another man. For it to be Rondo's bitch ass got to me even more. I have been losing shit to him my whole life, first my daddy, then the streets and the worst of all was Char. Now his ass was taken my money on the blacktop. I wanted his ass gone, but death was too good for him. I needed him to suffer, suffer like me.

I don't know how I ended up here, I was just driving, and something led me here. I hadn't talked to her in I don't know how long but here I was. When Char left me back then, she hopped right on to Rondo's dick, and I was hoping she was in the mood to do the same thing this time because I was willing and waiting. I hesitated, then said fuck it and got out of the car. The minute I walked into the shop all eyes were on me.

"What the hell are you doing here Noble?" Char said the minute she saw me walk in.

"I can't come and see an old friend?" I held my hands out in a playful way hoping to lighten the situation.

"Cut the shit Noble, what the fuck do you want?"

"I just want to talk to you."

She gave me a look and then looked down at her client and asked her to give her a minute. Once the client gave her the okay, Char took off her apron and headed in my direction. I couldn't help but noticed how thick she had gotten since I was with her. The sway of her hips created its own beat, and I was damn sure rocking to it. She pointed to the door in a nasty way which caused me to chuckle, I knew she was pissed, but I was a man on a mission. She walked past me, and I couldn't help but look at her ass. The minute we reached outside she turned to me and put her hands on her hips.

"Look I'm not for the shit today, what the fuck do you want?"

"I just wanted to see how you were, I knew things got crazy when we were in Farmington. I wanted to make sure that you were okay, that's all."

"Yeah, yeah I'm sure you got what you wanted." She wasn't falling for my bullshit, and I thought it was cute. She just didn't know that she was gone need some companionship soon, very soon.

"I just miss your friendship."

"Look, Noble, me and Rondo might be going through some shit but you know as good as anybody else I'm loyal, so that ain't opening the door for you to come in. And even if there was a chance that I was looking elsewhere you damn sure wouldn't be an option."

"Funny because you weren't very loyal to me." I raised my brows.

"Muthafucka the word loyal shouldn't ever come out of your mouth because if the shit doesn't benefit Noble, you don't give a fuck. My loyalty ended the day I walked in on you and Saniya, where the fuck is she anyway? Do she know you around here harassing folks?" she smirked, and I turned my head to spit because I suddenly got a bad taste in my mouth. "Hmmm I didn't think so, good bye Noble."

She turned to walk away, and I grabbed her arm, I was over her little nasty ass attitude. When she tried to jerk away, I gripped her arm tighter. I didn't know who the fuck she thought I was but I was far from the little nigga that used to chase behind her little stuck up ass.

Click Click, "You got two muthafucking seconds to get ya got damn hands off my woman before I splatter yo shit on this got damn side walk." I heard Rondo growl. I didn't even hear his ass pull up.

I let her arm go and held my hands up in surrender. I turned to him with a smirk on my face. I knew he wouldn't shoot me out here, it was too many witnesses. His gun was trained at my head as we stared each other down.

"I just came to make sure she was okay."

"Muthafucka, what does anything going on with her got to do with you?" he said through clenched teeth.

"Rondo please." Char grabbed his arm. "This is my shop." She reasoned, and it took him a minute, but he finally lowered the gun. She exhaled a sigh of relief, but that shit was short lived because that muthafucka snuck my ass. He hit me so hard I hit the ground. I looked up at him, and the look of hatred that poured from his eyes was mutual. I hated his ass just as much as he hated me. "RONDO!" Char yelled as he prepared to hit me again.

I wiped the blood that I felt drop from my lip with the back of my hand. I smiled and got up from the ground. I dusted my clothes off and adjusted the hat that I wore. I looked at her and then at him and nodded my head.

"Aight Bruh, you got that one."

"Yo ass gone have more than this if you don't stay the fuck away from Char." He seethed.

"Yo day is coming my brother." I backed away, and he started after me, but Char grabbed him.

"Bitch I'll be waiting."

I walked away and headed to my car. Once I got in, I burnt out away from the curb almost hitting a car that was coming. That was the last time these muthafuckas were going to disrespect me. I was about to make their lives a living hell, and they didn't even fucking know it. I picked up my phone to get shit popping.

"Hello," Ryan answered on the first ring.

"It's time nigga."

"When?"

"They gotta race Saturday."

"Aight." Was all he said. His bitch ass was starting to piss me the fuck off.

"Meet me at the fucking warehouse so we can handle this shit, we got one chance, and we needed to do this shit right." I didn't wait for him to respond I just hung up the phone, these niggas was gone be out of my got damn hair in no time.

ZAN

I don't know what the fuck Neala's problem was, I hadn't really talked to her since the night Tash came over there showing her ass and got her ass beat. I didn't think that Neala had all that in her, yeah, she talked a big game but I didn't know she could back that shit up. Seeing that made me want her little mean ass even more.

I had never clicked with someone like I click with Neala. It's like I can be myself around her no matter how rude or silly I am, she's good with it. Our conversations flow and her ass be having me feeling like a bitch, talking about the future and shit. I cussed her ass out about that one night, gone ask me where did I see myself in five years and I went to answer and scared my got damn self. Thugs don't do that shit.

Neala was a once in a lifetime chick, which I why I had stopped fucking with other bitches outside of my dumb ass baby mama. I know I should leave the bitch alone but she was convenient. The minute Neala admits this is what she wants then Tasha can kiss this dick goodbye, real talk.

Never in a million years would I have thought that I would be thinking about settling down but a nigga was ready to be sitting at home with Neala eating Captain Crunch and shit on Saturday mornings. I don't know what the hell that has to do with being in a relationship but it just sounds like something that you would do.

Seeing as though she wasn't answering my calls and shit, I decided to just pop-up on her ass. Her Instagram said that she was getting ready for her art show at a gallery uptown, so I grabbed up Z2, and we went to pay her a visit. I knew she was pissed at me and Z2 would soften the blow a little.

"Daddy? We going?" Z2 was only two, but he could talk good. He was still working on making out full sentences, but you could tell what he was saying.

"To see daddy friend Neala."

"Ne—Na" he was trying to say her name and couldn't, he was about to get pissed.

"Ne-la" I watched as he folded his arms in the rearview mirror, I could tell he was getting pissed because he couldn't say it. Finally, he sighed.

"Nene."

"Yeah, baby Nene." I laughed, he was definitely my son.

Pulling up to the gallery, I put money in the toll and grabbed Z2 out of the car. Grabbing his hand, so his little ass didn't run off, we walked in. Neala was standing on a ladder putting a painting on the wall. I could see that she had her headphones in her ears, so I just took a minute to sit back and admire her beauty. She was someone that I could see myself with.

"Nene!" Z2 yelled, and she looked towards the door. "Nene, right here."

She turned towards us and smiled at Z2 and then rolled her eyes at me and I chuckled. She was still a little pissed, but I was getting ready to dead all that shit. Climbing down off the ladder, she kneeled in from of Z2 and kissed him on the cheek.

"Z2 you trying to steal my woman, lil nigga." I hit him in the back of the head.

"Ha like me, daddy." The little nigga gone have the nerve to say.

"Ol' cock blocking ass." Neala pushed me in the shoulder and shook her head.

"Cock bwocking?" The confused look on his face was priceless.

"Yeah man that's when daddy trying to get some puss—"

"Zan!" Neala yelled.

"What I need him to know that he can't be in the way when daddy trying to do his thing."

"You got issues, what are you doing here anyway?"

"You won't answer your got damn phone, so I decided to pop the hell up."

"Well, I just saw you last night when you broke into my damn house."

"How the hell I break in, and I got a got damn key?"

"A key that I didn't give you."

"Look I ain't trying to hear all that, get ya shit and let's go."

"Where we going."

"None of ya got damn business just do what the fuck I said."

With that, I just walked out the door. I didn't have time to sit there and argue with her about dumb shit. I was stepping outside of my element already. A nigga didn't do shit like this, I didn't have to, but here I was. Plus, I needed to make up for that shit that Tash pulled even though I didn't have shit to do with what she did, she was a grown ass woman.

Me and Z2 got in the car and waited for about ten minutes, and she still hadn't come out. I shot her a text.

Me: If you don't bring your ass out of there I'ma come in there and show my ass.

I put my phone back in my pocket and not two minutes later she was coming out of the gallery. I smiled at the mug that was on her face, I didn't give a shit about that. I just wanted to spend some time with her and Z2; she needed to get used to being around him.

Shit was funny as hell because I had no intentions on doing anything with her except fucking, but I looked forward to seeing her ass even if she was sitting here with a sour look on her face. I knew that the only way that I would be able to make shit work with her is to let Tasha go, and I didn't have a problem with that, but I wanted to make sure that she was serious and ready so until then shit was going to be what it was.

Pulling up to the lake I got out, and she sat there with her arms folded and lips poked out. I got Z2 out of the car and walked off leaving her sitting there sulking. She would eventually get out cause I took the damn keys and the windows were up.

My ass felt like one of them fruitcake ass niggas, I was out here spreading blankets and shit, carrying picnic baskets. I kept looking around to make sure no one I knew was here because I wasn't trying to lose my street creds. I got everything ready for her mean ass and sat down on the blanket while Z2 ran off to play. Right as I pulled out my phone to call her stubborn ass, she walked up.

"What's all this?" she asked trying not to smile.

"Why you gotta be so hard all the time." I grabbed her arm and pulled her into my lap. "A nigga just wanna spend some time with ya."

"Awww you getting soft on me." I pushed her little ass right out of my lap she got on my got damn nerves. Try and do something good and she wanna run her mouth. She laughed and tried to climb back in my lap, and I blocked her. "Stop Zan shit, and if you push me again I'ma slap the shit out of you."

I wrapped my arms around her after she got comfortable back in my lap. I rested my chin on her shoulder and just looked out at the lake. The shit was so calming, I see why moms said to bring her here. Yeah, I had to get moms to help me out with this shit, you know my ass ain't come up with no shit like this.

"This is beautiful." She said and then sighed.

"What's on your mind?"

"Nothing." She relaxed against my chest.

"You know how the fuck I feel about lying right?"

"Why are you doing this Zan?" she slightly turned her body so that she could look at me.

"Because I wanted to, shit, what the fuck you mean." She rolled her eyes and tried to get up, I grabbed her. "Aight, man look I don't know what this shit is. I can't explain this shit at all I just know this is what I want right here, right now. Me, you, my son and this nasty ass lake." I scrunched my nose up. "Shit getting real for me."

"I'm not ready." She blurted out.

"Lying again." I looked her in the eye, and I could see that she was scared, she broke the stare and directed her attention to the play area where Z2 was calling her name asking her to come play with him. "Cock blocking ass little nigga, we gone talk about this shit."

"Leave him alone." She chuckled. "I don't know if I can deal with Tasha. The other night was a bit much, and I got too much to lose."

"I'll handle Tasha."

"Yeah, that's the problem you *handling* Tasha."

"That can all end with you."

"So, you still fucking her?" she asked with an attitude.

"Yep." Was all I said because it was the truth. "She the only one though besides you." I lightly headbutted her. "All you gotta do is say you're mine and that's it, it's a wrap."

"It don't work like that Zan, I need to see that you're serious about this. How can I do that if you still fucking yo crazy ass baby mama?" she shook her head. "I can't handle that, my heart can't handle that," she said lowly and that was the first time I really saw her vulnerable outside of the night she told me about her ex. I knew right then and there what I needed to do.

"Okay."

"Okay, what."

"I'm done fucking with Tasha."

"I'll believe it when I see it." she got up and ran over to where an impatient Z2 was waiting. I leaned back on my elbows and watched them play on the playground. I couldn't help but smile, this is what I wanted, and I was gonna have it. Neala looked at me while she was helping Z2 across the monkey bars, I blew her a kiss and smirked. Getting rid of Tasha was about to be a task , but it's what I needed to do.

"Damn a nigga is getting soft," I said to myself as I got up to go and join them in the play area. This was about to be my life, and I can't say that I was upset about it.

"Did you have fun today lil man?" I asked Z2 as we were walking up to the door at his house.

"With Nene?"

"What about me? You didn't have fun with daddy? Just Nene huh?" he laughed but he damn sure didn't say I was wrong.

"I stay with you."

"Not tonight baby. Daddy got business to handle." He puffed out his little chest and crossed his arms across it. I shook my head and laughed.

"Cock bwok" I had to laugh his ass didn't forget shit. I

knocked on the door instead of using the key I had. It was the first step in separating myself from her.

"Why in the hell you knocking and you got a key Zan?" she fussed and then bent down and kissed Z2 on the cheek. "Go get ready for bed man, me and daddy will be in to kiss you goodnight." I watched as he headed in the back to his room. I looked at Tasha who was dressed in a night robe, and I can almost guarantee that she didn't have shit on up under it. "You not coming in?"

I took a deep breath and stepped inside the house. "Yo, we need to rap about something."

"Sit down Zan. What the fuck is wrong with you? Why you acting all weird?" Her face had healed up good, but she had a scar on the right side of her face that I was sure wasn't leaving. Neala's ass did a number on her and to tell the truth, her ass deserved it.

"Call Nene call Nene." Z2 came running back in the living room in his Spiderman pajamas. I knew right then this conversation was about to go left.

"Who the fuck is Nene and why does my son want to call her?"

"Give daddy some dap dude, I'll see you tomorrow." I dapped my son up, and he frowned. "What's up man?"

"I call Nene." I hated that his mother was ignorant at that moment, he really wanted to call Neala, they really hit it off, and I had to tell my son no.

"Not right now dude."

"Why?"

"Cause ya mama ignorant and she ain't gone let you talk in peace." I didn't lie and I damn sure didn't lie to my son. He knew there wasn't no got damn Santa Clause, Tooth fairy or none of that shit. All that was daddy.

"Oh my God I hate you," Tasha said under her breath.

"We'll see Nene another time."

"No the hell you won't." Tasha interjected.

"Oh, mama ignant!" Z2 said trying to copy what I said. He started crying and took off towards the back. I got up to go after him, and Tasha grabbed my arm. I jerked away from her and gave her a look that told her to back the fuck up. I walked to the back room where Z2 was thrown across the bed having a mini melt down.

"What I tell you about crying son?" I turned him over and sat down beside him. He sat up and dried his face.

"Bitches cry."

"That's right! Are you a bitch?" He shook his head, I doubt he knew what the word meant but as long as he knew he wasn't one was good enough for me at the moment. "Alright then you'll see Nene again I promise and what daddy tell you about promises?"

"Daddy don't break promises."

"That's right son." I kissed his head and tucked him in the bed. I grabbed the remote and turned it on Paw Patrol, Tasha had about fifty episodes recorded, so he was set for the night. "I'll see tomorrow."

"Love you, daddy."

"Love you more son." I smiled back at him, I turned off the

light and shut the door because I knew this shit was about to get ugly.

Walking out of the room, I took a deep breath to try and calm down so I wouldn't choke her dumb ass. When I got back in the living room she was standing in the same spot that I left her in staring a hole through my ass, but I didn't give a fuck, I came here to do one thing and one thing only.

"What the fuck Zan? You ain't never did no shit like this until this little nappy headed bitch came around." She was on the brink of tears and I kind of felt bad for her.

"I'm feeling her Tash, I'm trying to make that shit happen."

"Wow!"

"You know I ain't gone lie about that shit," I shrugged. "She good people."

"Do you see what she did to my face and you talking about she good peoples?"

"Don't act dumb Tash, you came to that girl house acting a damn fool and she whooped yo ass. You deserved that shit and so much more. Don't play that role."

"What about me Zan?"

"I will always have love for you. You gave me my son but all this," I motioned towards her attire, "has to stop, I ain't fucking with you no more."

She looked at me like I was crazy and then slowly started to undo her robe. I shook my head feverishly because I knew that my self-control wasn't quite where I needed it to be. I cared about Neala, and I wanted to work some shit out with her, but we were at the beginning stages so I hadn't gotten to that point where I could control my dick especially around Tasha.

"Cut that shit out Tasha." She laughed.

"You gone leave all this alone?" She was now ass naked and looking at me with her eyebrows raised.

"Damn it, Tash, no I can't." I walked to the door which she stood in front of. She grabbed my hands and placed it on her pussy. Out of habit, I dipped a finger in, as usual, she was wet as hell. I bit my bottom lip. "This the last fucking time and I mean that shit." I was talking more to myself than her. I strapped up and did what I do best, fucked the sit out of Tasha to shut her the fuck up.

KY

I scooped Zan up so we could go and make this run. I still dabbled in the drug game but that's all I did was dabble. Every now and then I would have to make a run, but that was rare. Normally I just sat back and collected my money unless there was an issue that I needed to handle. The nigga that was supposed to go tonight, his girl was having their baby, and I wasn't a cold-hearted muthafucka, I understood family meant something. So, me and Zan headed to Georgia.

"Why the hell you looking all pissed off," I asked Zan who had barely said two fucking words since I picked his ass up. That wasn't him, that nigga talked all the got damn time.

"Tasha getting on my got damn nerves being childish and shit. Talking about I can't have Z2 around Neala anymore."

"I told you this shit was gone happen, you should have let

that shit go a long ass time ago nigga. Yo muthafucking ass don't listen. Now you feeling Neala and Tasha gone fuck that shit up."

"Man, you have no idea."

"What the fuck happened?"

"Neala told me she wasn't paying me no attention until I stopped fucking with Tash."

"And did you." He didn't say shit. "Nigga, aight!"

"Man, I fucked her a couple of times since then, but I told her ass I was done for real and that's when she started that bullshit."

"You ain't never gone shake that bitch, you may as well be with her." I was talking real shit because they had been doing this since she found out she was pregnant but Zan ain't never had no one he wanted to be serious with so her acting out didn't matter. Now he had Neala, he couldn't shake her dumb ass.

"Fuck you. Tash a project bitch, can't do shit with that."

"But keep fucking her right?"

"Man whatever."

"I don't wanna hear yo ass crying when she stops fucking with yo ass."

"She ain't going nowhere, not healthy anyway." He chuckled.

"The fuck is that supposed to mean?"

"Shit she gone be missing a limb or something I be damn if she walks off into the sun with another nigga, nah can't have that."

I laughed because to know Zan, you know that he don't ever talk like this. He don't give a fuck about females, it's not in his nature. So for him to be talking about chopping mutha-fuckas up is something serious. I kinda felt sorry for Neala because she was stuck with his unstable ass whether she wanted to be or not.

My phone rang, and I saw that it was Lovey, she had been calling since I called her about her being at Simon office. I knew that shit was a mistake. Now she pressuring a nigga into seeing her. I wanted to do that shit so she would leave my ass alone. I looked over at Zan, and he was mugging the shit out of me, I take it he saw who was calling my phone.

"Muthafucka, you sitting here trying to Dr. Phil my ass and here you are fucking with the Devil herself." His voice was a little louder than I preferred.

"You can calm yo ass down though."

"Fuck you!"

"Nigga fuck you, it ain't even like that."

"It ain't even like that." he mocked me. "Bullshit I saw the way you looked at that bitch. You dumb ass hell if you go back. That bitch took everything you had and left yo ass high and muthafucking dry."

"Nigga, don't you think I know that?"

"So what the fuck you talking to her aggravating ass for?"

"Got damn Zan you acting like you my bitch or something. What the fuck!"

"Bitch ass nigga I'll punch you all in yo shit."

I laughed and turned the music up, the conversation was over as far as I was concerned. I knew that Lovey was bad news and I was really starting to fall for Asta, but a part of me needed closure from Lovey. I wouldn't admit that shit to Zan bitch ass because I didn't wanna hear that shit.

Shit with Lovey and me ended so abruptly, and it deserves a conversation. It wouldn't change shit, I knew that she was no good for me. Asta had come in and taken up all the space that she left empty, so I was okay to have dinner with her. I didn't see anything wrong with it.

The rest of the ride was quiet, we did the pickup and drop off. I took him back to his crib, and I went back to mine. I hadn't really talked to Asta since I walked out of the radio station. I shot her a text.

Me: I miss you.

Beautiful: I can't tell.

I smiled at the text, I hopped out of bed and threw my shit back on. I headed over to her and Neala's crib, I wasn't surprised when I saw Zan pulling up the same time I was. He looked at me and shook his head, I flipped his bitch ass off and walked in after him. I went straight back to Asta's room.

She was laying on the bed in one of my t-shirts that I left over there and when I saw that was all she had on I shut and locked the door and undressed myself.

"Well hello stranger." I didn't say anything. She said she couldn't tell that I missed her, so I was about to show her just how much I missed her.

Climbing in the bed I hovered over her body and connecting with her lips, I slid my hand down until I was at her neatly shaven pussy. My finger took a dip into her wetness that was pooling around her center. Her hands found a home around my neck, and she pulled me closer to deepen our kiss.

"Mmmm" she moaned against my lips as I slowly moved in and out of her with expertise. "Shit!"

I continued to work my magic with my fingers. I knew she was almost at her peak when she started to grind down on my hand. I took my thumb and pressed it against her clit until I felt her pussy clench down on my fingers and her legs shake. Her eyes had rolled into the back of her head. When I felt like she was done with that orgasm I pulled my fingers out, and they immediately found my mouth. I licked them clean, she tasted just as sweet as the first time I attacked her ass in the office at the shop.

My eyes connected with hers and I felt something I hadn't felt in a long time. I kept trying to tell myself that three months is not enough time to love somebody, but I couldn't deny how I felt. She came in and turned shit all upside down but I wasn't complaining, I knew that she was worth it.

The bedroom was my specialty, and I was a nasty ass nigga, but tonight I needed to look into her eyes while I explained how I felt. I placed my dick at her opening and slowly slid into my heaven. She gasped as I went as deep as I possibly could. I kissed her deep and hard as I slowly moved my length in and out of her. She quickly caught rhythm with me, our bodies were in sync it was like we were making music of our own.

"Hey." I finally said as I worked my way around her pussy.

"Sweet Jesus." She said as she continued to roll her hips underneath me.

"So you don't wanna talk now."

"Ummm sshit." She moaned.

"You don't hear me talking to you Asta?" I whispered in her ear. She nodded and bit her lip. "You not gone talk to me." I sped up a little bit, and it was driving her crazy, I could tell by the way she was digging her nails into my skin. "My baby like that huh?"

"Yes baby" she moaned.

"Yes, baby what?" I taunted.

"Ummm I love it."

"Oh yeah." I bit my lip and grinded into her pussy, and that was a damn mistake because I felt my nut building up. I leaned up a little and started moving in and out of her at an even pace.

"I'm about to cum baby shit do that."

"Like this." I sped up.

"Yes yes yes yes ohhh yes." She was loud as fuck, but I didn't give a fuck. That let me know that I was doing what the fuck I was supposed to be doing. After a few more minutes of her choking the shit out of my dick, I was filling up her womb with my seeds.

I rolled off to the side of her, trying to get my breathing under control. She was sprawled out on the bed, the moon was shining right in her window and landed perfectly on her skin. It made her look like some kind of goddess. I knew right then and there, what I wanted to do. The room was quiet besides our breathing. I rolled over and pulled her to me.

"I love you, Asta." She froze up and if I wasn't mistaken, her ass stopped breathing for a minute. "Not just because you got A1 pussy but because I do." she cuddled up closer to me and threw her head back, I could see a lone tear roll down.

"Ky, I love you too." She whispered. "Don't hurt me."

I didn't say anything, I lifted her leg and entered her from behind. Nothing else needed to be said. This was about to be something beautiful. I wasn't about to let anyone mess this up, damn sure not Lovey.

~

Walking into Essex Bar and Bistro on S. Tryon, had me feeling like I was doing something wrong. Maybe I should have told Asta that I was coming here, but I wasn't doing anything just having a conversation. I took a deep breath and gave the hostess my name, she escorted me to my table.

I could feel someone watching me, I took a look around the restaurant but I didn't see anyone, so I pulled out my phone to shoot Asta a text to tell her to have a good time tonight and behave. They were taking Char out, Rondo wasn't happy about that shit, but honestly, he had no say so in much concerning Char nowadays.

"I'm glad you came," Lovey said as she walked up to the table. I looked up at her and had to tell myself to stop fucking drooling. She was dressed in one of those see through dresses, where you could see the panties and bra. She looked absolutely amazing and I wouldn't deny that but other than physically, she didn't move me.

"What's up Lovey." Was all I said and she laughed.

"You like my dress?" She got up and turned around real slow. "I thought about you when I bought it."

"It looks good on you, but this ain't what we here for." I looked at her, and she smacked her lips and sat down.

"Why you gotta be so cold."

"You really want me to answer that?" I raised a brow.

"If you're gonna act like this then we should just cancel this whole thing." Her attitude was evident, but I didn't give a fuck about that. She fucked me over, not the other way around. I was good to her, and she did me like that, and she just wants me to forget about that shit? I could never forget about that.

"Aight cool I'm out." I stood up and was about to leave until he grabbed my wrist. I looked down at her hand on me, and she snatched hers back.

"Okay. I'm sorry. You're right. We're here to talk about what happened."

I shot her a warning look. If she tried that bullshit again, I was out, and I meant it. I returned to my seat and ordered me a Henny and Coke, I was gone need it. This conversation was not gone be good.

"You really like her don't you?" she said sadly.

"Nah, I love that woman."

"How when you've only known her for a few months? How can you already love her?"

"When you know you just know." I shrugged my shoulders. "But this ain't about Asta."

"You right," she nodded and took a sip of the fruity ass drink she just ordered. "So she was the reason for all the shit at the office."

"I thought we weren't talking about Asta." I threw myself

back against the chair to show my frustration with her fixation on Asta.

"I'm just asking because I got grilled about my relationship with you after you left." She looked at me like I owed her something.

"And, that ain't got shit to do with me. Tell 'em the truth. We ain't got no relationship, we used to be together years ago, you were a grimy bitch that bounced on a nigga and took all my shit. That's all there is to it."

"I deserve that." she nodded.

"Man, what the fuck is this about?" I was starting to regret coming here. True I felt that I needed closure, I just wanted to know why but at this point does the shit even matter. "You know what." I stood up to leave again.

"I was pregnant." I stopped in my tracks.

"Say what now?" I could feel the anger creeping up through my fucking toes, it was too many witnesses in here to kill this bitch. "What the fuck you mean you *were* pregnant?"

"The baby was stillborn."

I hit the table hard as fuck with my hands, and she jumped. I balled my fist up and had to force myself to put my hands under the table. I didn't believe in putting my hands on a woman, and if I ever got to the point where I felt the need to, I would just walk away. Right now, I wanted to watch the life leave her eyes.

"You couldn't tell me that Lovey, I called yo ass for months!" I yelled louder than I wanted to.

"I didn't know how to, and I knew you would have wanted me to come back, and we raise the baby together."

"You got damn right Lovey you know how I feel about that shit."

I grew up in a two-parent household, me and my sister grew up with love and all that shit. I always said if I had kids, that's what I wanted for them and I would do whatever I needed to do to make that happen. If I had known Lovey was pregnant, I would have done a little more to find her and make shit right.

"I didn't want to struggle with a baby. I was gone have an abortion, but my mama made me keep it."

"I can't fucking believe you; you couldn't even tell me that my baby died?"

"I knew you would be pissed."

"You are a selfish bitch! You know that this whole fucking conversation been about you. You don't give a fuck about anyone but your got damn self. Yo ass leaving was the best got damn thing you could have done for me."

"I'm sorry, I just couldn't. You were so into this racing shit, we would've been broke!" she yelled.

I shook my head and looked at her. "Money over a family? Damn, I didn't think it was that bad." I let the hurt I was feeling pour out in my words, I didn't even care at this point.

"I—I."

"I nothing, Check it, stay the fuck away from me. I came here because I needed closure so I could fully move on with Asta and you just gave me that shit. I don't want shit to do with you and yo money hungry ass." I started to walk off, but I wasn't done. "But yo ass look stupid, a nigga got more money than I know what to do with. I bet yo ass feel dumb as fuck don't you?" I whispered that last part in her ear. "Keep the fuck away from me if you wanna keep breathing."

I looked at her one more time before I walked out of the restaurant. If I didn't hate that bitch before, I hated her right now. My head was all fucked up, and I had to go and meet Rondo and Zan, we had an "off the books" race tonight.

Its where we block off a section of the road and raced. This is where we made the most money, but tonight I didn't even know if I could concentrate long enough to do what I needed to do.

ASTA

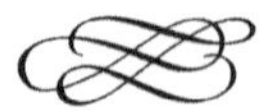

I was on cloud nine, ever since Ky told me that he loved me I hadn't stopped smiling. I was so shocked when he said it, I knew he cared for me because he showed me in the way that he treated me, but I didn't know he was there. I had never had a man be so attentive and caring, he noticed things about me before I did. He studies my body language and facial expressions, and he moved accordingly. I knew that I loved Ky the day that I told Simon about us, and to know that he felt the same way made my heart happy.

Looking in the mirror I could see that I was getting a little thick, I'd blame it on love. You know they say you gain weight when you're in love. I'll take it and whatever else came with it. Things were finally starting to come together for me, I was happy and had the job of my dreams. I don't think that anything could bring me down off this high.

"Girl, what you in here cheesing about?" Char asked from my room door.

"Oh, nothing." I blushed like a little school girl.

"It don't look like nothing." She walked in and sat on the bed. Char had quickly become my best friend I could talk to her about anything and the same with for her. As bad as I wanted to rant and rave about my relationship with Ky I knew what she was going through and I just didn't feel comfortable doing that. "Ky is a good guy, I've known him since he was a little knuckle head running around the damn city like he ain't' have no got damn sense." She laughed, and I joined her. "Don't ever feel like you can't enjoy your happiness around me, I'm not that kinda person." She looked at me daring me to deny what she just said.

"I know it's just I know what you are going through."

"Girl that don't matter, I'm happy for you no matter what storm I'm going through. Me and Rondo will fight our demons don't worry about us." She waved me off. "Regardless of what we go through I'm your friend, so that means you can tell me anything." She smiled.

That's why I loved her, damn near the whole world came crashing down around her and she still ready to be here for me. I wanted to kick Rondo's ass for her. Shit sucked because she was such a good person with a good heart. I hope for her sake that it's not his baby.

"Well, in that case, I'm falling head over heels for that nigga with his black ass."

"That nigga is black," Neala said joining the conversation.

"Shut the hell up, don't worry about him. Worry about Zan's aggravating ass." She rolled her eyes and smirked.

"Awww look at y'all." Char put her hand over her mouth pretending to be emotional. "I remember the day I fell for Rondo. I had just got out of a relationship with Noble's hoe ass. You talking about a dog, that nigga broke the damn mold. He had bitches everywhere, and my ass rode that shit out with him. It wasn't until I caught him with my best friend that I said enough was enough." She shook her head. "I ran into Rondo, the same day I caught them. I was crying in the park, and he sat down and asked me why I was crying. We sat at that park and talked until the sun came up and we've been together ever since. It was like that man was heaven sent." She smiled and then looked up at the sky and her sky faded as her reality kicked in. "Now I just wanna throw the whole nigga away." We laughed. "God, I think you made a mistake, shit!"

"I love how with all of this you never lost who you were," I told her.

She shrugged, "People go through shit. Now that I've had a chance to calm down, I realize that technically he didn't cheat. I broke up with him, but I still feel like the shit was wrong, it wasn't the first time we had argued and said some shit we didn't mean. He was looking for a reason to do some single shit, and I gave it to him."

"It's not your fault," Neala said with her hands on her hips.

"Chile, I know that, that's all him."

"What you gone do if the baby his?" I asked.

"That's something that I don't know. I wanna be able to say

that I would accept the baby with open arms, but I would be lying if I did." we both just nodded. "I guess we'll have to see, but right now I don't wanna talk about this shit. I wanna go out and have a damn good time."

"Turn up then." Neala said and started twerking on the bed. We laughed at her ass, and I finished getting dressed so we could leave.

I had settled on a simple black t-shirt dress with these cute ass black booties that I ordered from Just Fab for $39.95. I loved a good bargain. Neala wore a cute ass red, short romper that barely covered her ass. Char was cute with some khaki shorts on with a see through top and khaki colored bra. We were casual, but we made the shit look good.

We headed out a little after ten, we wanted to get to club Vibrations before all the VIP sections were taking. I was not about to be in no club without VIP, I just couldn't do it.

Stepping into the club, the vibe was chill and the music was on point. I loved going to this club because it played a mixture of new school and old school music, the food was good and the drinks were strong. We secured our VIP and ordered a bottle, tonight was about to epic and I was ready to enjoy that shit with my girls.

"Ayyye." I heard Neala yell over the music the minute she heard Taking over for the 99 and the 2000. She grabbed our hands, and we all headed for the dance floor and tore that shit up.

We had a little circle in the middle of the dance floor, I hadn't really partied with Char before so I didn't know how she acted on the party scene but she showed me real quick. She could dance her ass off, she was getting it. A fine ass dude walked up behind her and started dancing with her I just knew she was gone ask him to move but she started dancing harder. For some reason I looked around, I guess making sure Rondo wasn't gone pop the hell up. She told us he didn't really like that fact that she was going out.

"Go Char." Neala cheered her on while she was bent over in front of some guy that she had snatched up. I laughed at them and started twerking on the dude that had come up behind me. I didn't see anything wrong with it, hell we were just dancing.

We danced for a good ten songs before we all headed back up to VIP to regroup. We all fixed a few drinks and really started to turn up. I had just poured my third shot when the girl that stopped us outside of Chima's that day walked up. I found out that it was his ex, even though I didn't want to know he still ended up telling me who she was and what she used to be to him. She looked me up and down, and I returned the gesture. I wasn't intimidated in the least; I was confident in my position.

"Asta right?" I smiled and nodded. "You're cute."

"I know." I was not about to give this bitch life when she wanted what I had.

"I can see why Ky is so wrapped up in you." I exhaled loudly to show my frustration.

"Who the fuck is this?" Neala said noticing my change in mood. When Char turned around, she smacked her lips and came and joined us.

"Char," Lovey said nonchalantly.

"Lovey." She countered.

"Again, who the fuck is this," Neala yelled this time.

"This is Ky's EX girlfriend."

"And you're here, why?" Neala looked around.

"I just wanted to say hey to the woman that was able to steal Ky's heart." She smirked.

"I didn't steal anything; it was given to me after you left him high and dry." I looked at her, and I guess what I said pissed her off because her body language became defensive. "Look I don't want no issues with you, you had him you left him, and I thank you for that. If you hadn't have done what you did, he wouldn't be the man he is to me." That honestly wasn't a dig; I meant that.

"Just tell him I said thanks for having dinner with me and I'm sorry." When she said that I could feel the anger brewing I wanted to smack that fucking smirk off her face, but I would never let another bitch see me sweat. I just smiled.

"I'll tell him tonight while I'm riding his ass to sleep." I winked, and she stomped off. Neala and Char high fived me. The minute she was out of sight I pulled out my phone and cussed him out.

Me: SO YOU SAYING YOU LOVE ME MEANS YOU GO OUT ON A DATE WITH YOUR EX? SHIT DON'T MAKE SENSE SMH

I didn't even wait for a response I knew he was at a race, so I didn't expect him to see it until later. I put my phone back in my bag and continued to drink my ass off. Mad was an understatement. I knew this shit was too good to be true.

NEALA

Char and Asta were drinking more than I could keep up with. I knew they both were hurting, I didn't want to be a Debbie downer or no shit like that, but these bitches were getting out of hand. Asta had some dude up in VIP talking and chilling like they belonged there and Char had been on the dance floor with the same nigga for about an hour.

I kept looking around for one of them niggas to pop the hell up. They were well known, so I'm sure somebody in this bitch knew who Char and Asta belonged too. The last thing I needed was for that psycho ass Ky and is crazy sidekick Zan to bust up in here swinging on people.

"Asta baby, let me holla at you." I tugged on her arm and smiled at ol boy who was staring at Asta like he was gone eat her ass up. "Um if Ky walks in this bitch and see that shit you and that nigga gone come up missing you know that right?"

"Fuck Ky, he can go on dates and shit, I can do me, right?"

"No bitch it don't work like that." she snatched away from me. "You know that hoe was just trying to get under your skin. Ky don't want her ass you know that." she ignored me, and I looked out on the dance floor to see if I can spot Char and I didn't see her. I looked to my left and saw that she was headed out the door with the mystery man. "Asta don't you fucking move." I pointed at her, and she waved me off and went back to the conversation she was having.

I ran out of VIP to go find this heffa. This was the last time that I was going out with their high-strung asses. Right as I turned the corner, I ran right into Pink. Fuck! Tonight, was not the night for this shit.

"So you just gone run right past me without saying anything."

"Not right now Pink, I gotta find my friend."

"It's always someone or something else that comes before Pink, right?"

"Man can we do this later." I was panicking because I didn't want Char going with that nigga and somebody that knows Rondo tell him that shit. I needed to get to her. I tried to get around Pink, and he blocked me. "Get the fuck out of my way!"

"Not til you talk to me."

"Not now," I pushed his ass out of the way and ran out the door. I looked around and didn't see her, then all of a sudden, I heard a big commotion on the side of the building. I ran that way, and I cussed myself for not trying harder to get them to chill. There stood Rondo, Zan, and Ky. I couldn't do nothing but shake my head. My first thought was to go warn my sister, but Char needed me at the moment.

“What the fuck you think you doing?” Rondo grabbed her arm, and she jerked away.

“Aye, nigga don’t be touching her like that.” Mystery man said putting his arm in front of Char. The look in all three of their eyes got dark as hell. I ran over and pulled Char, and she jerked away from me.

“No, I got this.” She slurred.

“I got her.” the Mystery man just didn’t know his got damn place, he couldn’t have been from here.

“Muthafucka if you wanna keep yo life I suggest you shut the fuck up before I gut yo ass.” Rondo gritted through clenched teeth.

“I don’t understand what your problem is,” Char yelled.

“So you just gone up and leave with some random ass nigga? That’s some hoe shit, Char.” Rondo was fuming, but he was trying his best to be patient with her. He knew she was acting out because she was hurt, but I could tell that she was pushing it.

“Yep, oh wait I forgot we gotta break up first. We done, it’s over, now it’s safe for me to fuck him and come back to you in the morning,” she smirked. “That’s what we do right?” she screamed.

“Ooou” I let out by accident. Char was on one, and this shit was about to get ugly and fast. “Char, baby let's just go.” I tried to reason with her, but she never broke her stare with Rondo.

“Let’s go, Char.” Rondo attempted to get her to see shit his way one more time. She crossed her arms across her chest and just stared at him like she was saying make me.

"Nigga you can go," Ky said calmly.

"Who gone make—"

Click click was all you heard before dude could even get his sentence out, Ky and Zan had their guns trained on him. That nigga didn't say shit else, he just stood there with his head up like Cuba Gooding Jr in Boys in the Hood when the cop pulled out on him.

"Bye," Zan said, and that nigga all but took off running.

Rondo walked up to Char, and she pushed him out of her face. She cussed out Zan and Ky right before Rondo picked her up and threw her over his shoulder and carried her ass to his car. He asked Zan and Ky were they okay and they nodded and turned to me. I looked around trying to avoid their stares, but it didn't help.

"What the hell you looking at me like that for, shit I can't control them heffas." I turned on my heels to try and get to my sister before Ky saw what she was doing, but Zan caught me by my shoulder.

"Don't even think about it, he already saw the shit." I narrowed my eyes at Zan and turned to Ky.

"Your little bitch paid her a visit and said some shit, and she pissed. Yall just need to talk."

He didn't comment on what I said nor did he look my way, he walked right passed my ass and headed for the club. The bouncer nodded at him and Zan and let them right in knowing they were both strapped. They had pull around Charlotte, and I just found out how much.

I tried to run in front of Ky, but Zan kept pulling me back. We fought back and forth for a minute. I walked right past Pink, and I prayed that he didn't say shit, he looked at me and then Zan and nodded. Zan missed that, and I was thankful.

Ky was a calm kinda crazy, so calm that the shit was scary. He walked right up in the section where Asta and ol'boy was sitting. She didn't even know that he was standing there she was so enthralled in her conversation, she didn't even realize that her life was in danger. Ky leaned over and lightly knocked over the cup that she was barely hanging on too, the contents of the cup landed in ol'boy's lap.

"What the fuck." He jumped up.

"I need to holla at my woman for a second," Ky said calmly but loud enough to be heard over the music. His eyes were staring holes through Asta, and this bitch gone have the nerve to look over at me. *Nah bitch, I tried to warn yo hard-headed self.* I just shook my head.

"Ky, I was just—" Ky held his hand up to stop her from talking, and she gasped and put her hands on her hips.

"Can you excuse us please?" Ky addressed the dude. I could see the damn steam coming out of his head.

"Nigga I ain't going—" was all ol' boy got out before his face met the butt of Ky's gun, blood went everywhere, and the people around us started screaming and scattering, Ky didn't flinch, his eyes were trained on his target.

"Bitch I asked you nicely, and I ain't gone ask again, I'm

perfectly fine with letting my shit go in this muthafucka." He growled, the guy grabbed his nose and looked at Ky. I could tell he was in pain, but Ky didn't give two fucks. Ky tilted his head as if he was daring to guy to sit there any longer.

"I'm so sorry," Asta said, and Ky gave her the ugliest look, and she backed up to where I was. "Bitch why didn't you warn me."

"Hoe I did, yo drunk ass knew everything. That shit sobered you up real quick huh?" she smacked her lips and looked on to see what the dude was gone do.

"I'm not one for many words," Ky said standing with his gun by his side. Shit was crazy because security had yet to come the fuck over there. Thank goodness, the dude took heed to the threat and got up and left. Ky walked over to where we were standing, and I just knew we were gone have to jump his big ass.

"See what you made me do." he looked at her as he cleaned the butt of his gun off with a napkin from one of the tables. Everybody that was around us was just looking at the big black crazy nigga to see what the fuck he was gone do next.

"What the fuck, you can have dinner dates and shit, and I can't have a conversation with the opposite sex?"

"It wasn't even like that. That's the fucking problem, you can't believe everything these bitches out here saying. You gone hear a lot of shit dealing with me, so what you gone pull this shit every time you get mad?" He waved his gun around VIP, and everybody started ducking, this nigga was unhinged. "If so it's gone be a lot of fucked up muthafuckas walking round here." he looked her in the eye. "When I told yo little I ass I loved you, I meant that shit. But what you ain't gone do is make a fool of me."

"And you ain't gone make one of me." Asta just needed to shut the hell up got damn. "Got yo ex coming up to me to tell me you were just with her. If it wasn't like that why didn't you tell me?" she asked.

"You right. I should have, but I told that bitch the same thing I'm saying now. That I love my woman but I ain't about to talk about this shit right now, let's go." he pointed to the exit and Asta turned on her heels and headed out, her ass pouted the whole way but she went.

"You get the hell out too," Zan said slapping me on the ass.

"Whatever." I laughed.

We walked out and when we got to the entrance where Pink was standing Zan let go of my hand. I just knew that he didn't see him, but I guess I was wrong. Zan stood right in front of him and rocked the shit out of him.

"Stay from round her," he yelled over the music, and we walked out hand and hand. "You thought I didn't see that nigga, didn't you?"

"I just didn't want no shit, I didn't say two words to him. I didn't even know he was here until I came out to find Char."

"Neala don't fucking play with me aight?"

"I should be telling you that," I said referring to his baby mama.

"Aye nigga." I heard Pink yell once we were outside. I said a silent prayer that he just went on about his way. Zan ass didn't have it all either. When we turned around Pink had a gun trained on Zan. "What now nigga." He taunted.

I watched as Ky drew his gun but Zan didn't. Instead, he laughed and walked right in the direction of where Pink was standing with his gun trained on him. My heart was beating because I didn't want anything to happen to Zan and his ass was walking around like he was invincible.

"Zan no." I cried as he walked right up on Pink's gun, the gun was metal to chest. He just stared at Pink while Pink was shaking and biting his lip. Ky had joined the party and had his gun to Pink's head.

"Don't ever pull no gun unless you plan on using it pussy," Zan growled. They stood there in a stare down for what seemed like forever, but in reality, it was only like thirty seconds. Then Pink finally lowered his gun. "That's what the fuck I thought." Zan turned around and grabbed my hand, and we walked to my car.

"You know we gone have to dead that nigga," Ky said like we weren't standing there.

"Yep" was all Zan said. I looked at Asta, and she looked at me, what the hell had we gotten ourselves into.

RONDO

The whole ride home I just kept looking over at Char, I knew that she was hurting, but she was definitely taking shit too far. I wanted to wake her drunk ass up so bad, but I took this time to calm down. She was just acting out how she felt I felt when I fucked Rachel, so I really couldn't be that mad. Once we pulled up at home, I slightly nudged her awake.

"Damn go on somewhere now I'm sleeping." She slurred.

"We're home, come on man."

She leaned her head over and the next thing I know I heard her snoring. I didn't give a fuck if she was drunk or not we were going to have this conversation. I got out of the car and walked around to her side, picked her up out of the car and through over my shoulder. I don't think I've ever seen Char this drunk.

"Just let me go to sleep Rondo damn," she slurred.

"Nah, I'm about to fix your ass some coffee. We need to talk about this shit, I can't live like this no more."

"You made this bed Rondo, now you gotta lay in it."

She started wiggling her way out of my arms, I was struggling to open the door and hold her at the same time. I finally got the front door open, and I walked over and dumped her on the couch. She looked up and narrowed her eyes at me, and I chuckled. Two of us could play his game tonight.

"You didn't have to throw me damn," she threw the pillow at my head. I turned around and looked at her, and she flipped me off.

"Well don't act like we didn't talk about this."

She smacked her lips and crossed her arms across her chest, and mumbled something under her breath. I tried my best not to get mad at her because I knew what part I have played in all of this, but she was making it really hard.

"Look, I know I fucked up, but enough is enough. We either gone talk about this shit and work through it, or we go our separate ways."

I knew I didn't have the right to make any ultimatums but living like this just wasn't healthy. We needed to come to some kind of resolve or we both were going to end up resenting each other. The look she gave me scared me because I didn't know if she was gonna say let's call it quits. Even though I just said we could go our separate ways, I don't know if I would be able to handle that. I was praying that she was gonna see things my way and we work this shit out.

"You got some damn nerve, don't come to me with that shit after everything you put me through."

"Got damn Char what do you want me to do? Okay yeah, I let my ego get in the way aight. I went out and fucked that bitch. Shit didn't mean nothing. I was just fucked up behind the shit you said." I pointed at her. "You think I meant to hurt you? Think about that shit, I've never given you a reason to doubt me, I've been loyal as fuck." I was so mad that I was spitting everywhere. "Baby, I don't know what else to do; you gotta tell me what to do."

"A baby?" She said looking up at me. "How can I compete with the baby."

I felt my heart drop to my stomach as I could hear the pain in her voice. I never wanted her to feel like she had to compete for my love, that was never the case and never will be the case. I love her too much for that. I just wish she understood that I made a mistake and it would never happen again.

"Baby you never have to compete for my heart because you own it."

"I don't think you understand how much this hurts, just thinking about you having what's supposed to be mine with someone else."

"But we don't even know—"

"But what if it is." Her voice trembled. The thought of me having a kid with someone else was slowly killing her. I would give anything to be able to give her that security that she needs right now but in reality, her worst fear may be coming true, and I hated myself for it. "And do you know that bitch came to my fucking shop?" Her hurt quickly became anger in a matter of seconds.

"What you mean she came to the shop?"

"Exactly what the fuck I said, that's what I'm not gone put up with. That's my place of business."

"Baby I know and I'm gone handle that shit, believe that." I seethed, that bitch just didn't know when to fucking quit.

"How in the hell you think shit gone be if that is ya baby? I will go to jail for choking that hoe out."

"It won't be like that Char, I can guarantee that."

"How Rondo? How can you guarantee that this bitch ain't gone be on no bullshit?"

"Because I can," I yelled unintentionally.

"Ugh, I need a drink." She rolled her eyes and tried to get up, but I stopped her and pulled her to me. It felt good because this is the closest that I've been to her since all the shit went down. When she didn't reject my touch, I took that as a green light to keep going. I press my lips against hers, and at first, she didn't reciprocate, but I didn't give up, I couldn't. After a while, she gave in and parted her lips, and for the first time in months, I felt connected to her.

"You don't know how much I love you Char."

"So why did you hurt me."

"I'm so sorry you will never know how sorry I am."

A picked her up, and she straddled my waist, I took no time getting into the bedroom. I didn't want her to change her mind. Being so close to her gave me hope that we could work things out. When we got to the bedroom I stood her on her feet, I looked at her to get permission for what I wanted to do next. She didn't say yes, but she didn't say no either.

I began to undress her, she just stood there staring off. Char was so sexual, and the fact that she wasn't participating, was fucking with me. I had something for that. Once she was undressed, I laid her down on the bed.

"I can't change the past but I can promise you that our future is secure, just tell me that you're gonna be here for that. I can't live without you, Char."

She didn't respond, but she didn't have to. No matter what I said about going separate ways, I knew for a fact that I needed her and I didn't want to live without her in my life. I prayed daily that this baby wasn't mine, but if it was, I just wanted her to know that it wouldn't end us if anything I would do what I needed to do to make sure that it made us stronger.

I got down on my knees and parted her pussy lips. I was about to paint my love all over her. When I was done, she was gone understand what she meant to me, and if God was on my side then I would be giving her the baby she wants tonight.

RYAN

"What the fuck am I doing riding around with 4 kilos of coke? Put myself in the middle of some beef that I got nothing to do with." I said looking at myself in my rearview mirror as I sat around the corner from the palace. I was starting to second-guess my decision to fuck with Noble and all this bullshit. I was already at odds with Rondo about Rachel, so the last thing I needed was for him to be at my head about the shit.

I had made a deal with the devil. So at this point, I didn't have a choice. Money was a powerful bitch, especially when you were trying to live your dreams. I took a few deep breaths and shook off any nervousness that I was feeling. I stepped out of the car and grabbed the duffel bag right as my phone began to ring. I looked at the screen and saw that it was Rachel calling, I shook my head and cleared her and dropped my phone in my pocket. I didn't have time for her bullshit today.

The palace was surrounded by woods so it was easy to go in the back. I had my homeboy Rall to leave it open for me, I told him that I had left some of my shit in there that I needed to get from a new gig. That was my boy, so he didn't question it, he just told me he had me. When I got to the back door just like he said, it was open. I walked in and headed to the office area.

My phone rang again, and I cussed myself for not putting it on silent. I pulled it out of my pocket prepared to cuss Rachel out because I just knew it was her, but to my surprise it was Noble. I don't know why the fuck he was calling me knowing what I had to do.

"Fuck you calling me for Noble?"

"Yo the race was cut short get the fuck out of there!"

"Fuck you mean the race was cut short?"

"Just what the fuck I said, if you want to live you will get the fuck out of there!"

"Fuck!"

I hung up on Noble and dropped my phone back in my pocket. I looked around frantically trying to figure out my next move; I knew I should have left the shit alone. The last thing I needed was them crazy ass niggas to catch me in here, I was sure I wouldn't make it out alive. Right as I made up my mind to get the hell out of there and say fuck all of this I heard a noise.

"Shit!"

"Zannnnnn I'm tired," I could hear a female whine.

"Chill Neala, I just gotta pick up this money." He told her, and I just stayed quiet.

Then it hit me that his ass was heading into the office. There was a door that lead to a small building on the side of the Palace where Rondo kept spare parts for the shop. I slipped back there and waited. My heart was beating hard as fuck, and I was trying to control my breathing. I looked around for an exit and didn't see one. I was just gone have to wait this one out.

"Aight girl, shit I got it." I heard him say after about three minutes and then I heard the door shut. I waited a few more minutes just to make sure that he was gone. I came out of the little building and listened to see if I heard him. When I didn't hear anything, I quietly slipped out of office and was on my way out the door when my phone started ringing again at the same time I could hear someone unlocking the door. I took off towards the back door.

Once the door was open Zan stood still for a second, it was dark, so he was probably trying to adjust his eyes, he took two steps, and the next thing I heard was a gunshot. I ducked and took off out the door. I could hear his footsteps closing in on me, but I just kept running. *Pow Pow*, I ducked again. *Pow*, "Fuck!" I yelled and grabbed my shoulder and ended up dropping the duffle bag with the drugs in it. I fucking forgot to leave the fucking bag, how did I forget to drop the got damn bag. I picked the bag up with my other arm, and I said a quick prayer to the man upstairs to help me out of this shit.

I got into the woods that surrounded the Palace and found a place to catch my breath. I looked around, and I didn't hear anything. My shoulder was hurting like a muthafucka, but I sucked that shit up. It was either take that shit or die, and I definitely didn't want to do that. I heard him step on a branch and I held my breath. Then I heard his phone ring.

"Yeah, I'm good, it was Ryan nigga." I immediately dropped my head, how in the hell did he know it was me? It was dark as fuck in there, how he see me? "He ran in the woods," he said as he continued to walk in my direction. "Aight, when I find that nigga he dead." I swallowed hard. "Aight I'm here, I'm about to see what the fuck that nigga was doing here. Yeah, tell Rondo bitch ass to get out of Char cat and come log into this security shit."

I stayed put, I could hear him still walking around, and I wasn't about to make any movements to cause attention to myself.

"Zan." I could hear the girl whisper. "You okay?"

"Yeah baby, I'm coming." His ass let off another round, and I could hear him walking away. I waited about five minutes, and then I eased out of the woods and back to my car. I didn't even bother to check my surroundings, I got in and threw the duffle bag in the seat and pulled the hell off. I picked up my phone and dialed Noble. I was scared as shit, and I knew that I was gone have to get out of town before these muthafuckas found me.

"Aye, you get out of there?"

"Fuck no, nigga I got shot! I knew this shit wasn't a good idea." I hit the steering wheel. "I told you this shit was a bad idea."

"Shut yo bitch ass up, just come to the warehouse."

"Fuck you, all this because yo ass got daddy issues. I knew I shouldn't have fucked with you." I fumed. "Oh shit," I said as I saw the blue lights behind me. "I'm getting fucking pulled."

"If you lose my dope." He growled.

"Oh for real that's all you give a fuck about? Fuck you." I hung up the phone and pulled over to the side of the road. I waited for the officer to come up to the window.

"License and registration please." The officer said, and I reached in the seat and got the information that he needed.

"Is there a problem officer?"

"Yeah, I saw you coming out of the woods back there with a duffle bag." He said looking in the car at the duffle bag. "And you were shot." He nodded at my shoulder. "On top of that, you were going 60 in a 35." I kicked myself for not watching my fucking surroundings.

"Sit tight." He told me as he called for an ambulance, I tried to tell him that I didn't need one, but he insisted. He also called for the K-9 unit. I knew I wasn't getting out of this now. I threw my head on the steering wheel.

I could hear the sound of a motorcycle near where we were. I looked up, and I knew right away that it was Ky's bike he was the only bike around her that color. It was dark, but you could see the silver and Carolina blue of the bike. I could see him lift his face mask and look me directly in the eye as he slowed down to ride by. I could see nothing but death in his eyes. I knew right then and there that I was fucked, either way, I was fucked.

ZAN

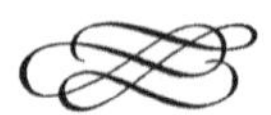

Pissed didn't even begin to describe what I was feeling right now. I was looking all around the Palace trying to see what the hell this muthafucka was here for. How in the hell did he get in here was the better question? Rondo had everything changed and had that security system put in after the police raided our shit. We were the only ones with access, so shit wasn't adding up.

"What the hell was that about?" Neala asked breaking me out of my thoughts.

"Shit I don't know, but you better believe I'm bout to find out." I could hear Ky pulling up. He started talking before he got in the building good.

"I just passed that bitch up the road."

"You dead that nigga?"

"Nah fool, the police had that shit on lock."

"Fuck man!"

"Did you see him leave with anything?" Ky asked.

"I don't fucking know nigga it was dark as fuck." he chuckled and shook his head. I shrugged my shoulders. "If Rondo's bitch ass don't climb out the pussy and come the hell on," I said as the doors open.

"Stay out of grown folk business lil nigga."

"First of all ain't shit little about me bitch, and second, look at you nigga." I cheesed. "A nigga got that pussy glow." He laughed, and so did Ky.

"What the fuck is a pussy glow?" he asked.

"When yo ass ain't had no pussy, and you finally hit some, a nigga lights the fuck up."

"Shut the fuck up." Ky and Rondo said in unison.

"Fuck yall, aye let's go check out that security shit." I nodded to the back and Rondo led the way.

We had cameras everywhere, but you wouldn't know it. He hit a few buttons, and we watched as that nigga came in through the back and headed to the office. He had a big ass duffle bag with him. I watched as I walked in on one camera and he dipped off and in the little room that we had in the back for spare parts. He hung around for a second but never touched anything or nothing. Whatever he was doing I interrupted him, and I was glad.

"What the fuck was you shooting at?" Rondo asked as he continued to watch the tape.

"We had an intruder, I was doing what the fuck I was supposed to do."

"Nigga yo ass missed" Rondo laughed.

"Ol' Barney Fife ass nigga," Ky said and then laughed. I pushed his ass, and he continued to laugh.

"Nah I hit that muthafucka, I heard his ass cry out before he hit the woods." I shrugged.

"Good I hope that muthafucka catch an infection and die," Rondo said.

"Fuck that, he gone catch these bullets," Ky said. "But check it, ain't shit we can do tonight if the police got his ass hemmed up. So I'm about to get back to the house, me and Asta got some shit to talk about."

"I hope y'all ass keep that shit down. Asta ass be in there howling and shit, be fucking up my rhythm. Can't even get in like I want to for thinking something gone bust through the door and eat my ass up."

"That's cause you a fuck boy, and you don't know what you doing, we at my crib anyway," Ky smirked, and Neala laughed.

"The fuck you laughing for? Ima fold yo ass up like a got damn pretzel." I pointed at her. "And you bitch, ask yo mama," I said and took off running towards the door because I knew his hostile ass was gone come after me.

We took one more look around to make sure shit was straight, once we were satisfied we all dipped out. Me and Neala were on our way to the house, laughing and talking about nothing. This was one of the things that made me want to make things permanent with her, there was never a dull moment between the two of us. We just clicked, and I was starting to realize that this was something that I didn't want to live without.

My phone rang for the 20th time today, and of course, it was

Tasha. I ignored it, as usual, Z2 was with mama, so it wasn't anything that I cared to talk about. I knew when I heard Neala sigh that shit was about to turn sour.

"You gone get that?" Neala asked with more attitude than I had patience for.

"Nope."

"Why not?"

"Why do I need to, it ain't nobody but Tasha's dumb ass wanting to get on my got damn nerves. Z2 wit my mama so what I need to talk to her for."

"You would be talking to her if I wasn't in the car with you though, wouldn't you."

"I only talk to Tasha if it's got something to do with Z2." I wasn't lying, that's the only time I talk to her. Now, when I get there and she starts her shit is when I end up fucking with her dumb ass.

"So you talking to her about Z2, ends up with you in her bed." Here we go, I thought.

"Neala do you really want me to answer that?" I asked her giving her a chance to just let the shit go.

"Fuck yeah, cause I'm about to be out if you can't control yo self around her. I know you will have to deal with her because she's the mother of your child, but damn. What's the use in me putting my all into you when you still fucking with her?"

"I told you all you got to say is that you're mine, that's it. It's fucking simple." I unintentionally raised my voice.

She smacked her lips and turned to face the window. The rest of the ride to the house was quiet. When we pulled up, I got out and sparked the blunt that I had in my pocket. I needed to mellow the fuck out before I walked in here. I walked to her side of the car and opened the door, she got out with an attitude. I tried to grab her hand, and she snatched away. I grabbed her again and then gave her look to let her know I wasn't with her shit tonight.

"So this is how it's gone be all night?" She didn't say anything, and I shook my head.

I was tired of playing this little game with her. I knew we said we were gonna see how shit went but I didn't want that shit, I wanted her. In order for me to have her in the way that I wanted, I needed to get rid of Tasha. That shit was easier said than done but I was gone have to do it.

~

"What's up mom dukes," I said as I let myself in the house and walked into the kitchen where she and Z2 were having breakfast.

"Hey, son." She said unenthusiastically.

I sighed. "Damn you too." I opened the refrigerator and pulled out of the orange juice and drank it out the carton because I knew that she hated when I did that. She slapped me in the back of my head, and I ended up spitting some of the juice out, she hit me again for getting shit on her floor. Z2 laughed. "What you laughing at little nigga?"

"Stop calling him that Zander!"

"Why, he is my little nigga. Ain't that right?" I walked over to dap him up, and he looked at my mom, and she looked at him. He just looked at me and smiled. "Damn homie she already got to you huh?" he nodded his head and I chuckled.

"That girl was at my house last night after midnight."

"Damn ma why didn't you call me?"

"Cause I handled it," she said and looked at me. I swallowed hard because I didn't want to know what she meant by that. Tricia Caldwell wasn't green to the streets; she was out there with my daddy when he did his thing so when she said she took care of it, that could mean a few different things. "I didn't kill the bitch." She said and covered her mouth and then looked at Z2. "I'm sorry baby, go play in your room while me and daddy talk." He hopped down and took off down the hall. That little nigga had two speeds, zero, when his ass was sleep and ten every second that his eyes were open.

"You could've called me, and I would have taken care of it, I told her dumb ass not to come back the fuck over here." I went to grab my phone to cuss her ass out.

"No Zander, this shit is your fault. You give that girl the power to do this shit. When you sleep with her, you make her ass think she is winning. She ain't never gone respect you or no one you ever deal with because don't give her nothing to respect son. Every time she shows her ass you go right over there and stick ya little ding-a-ling right in her."

"Ma—" I hated when she said shit like that. I mean damn I wasn't five no more.

"Shut the hell up boy, I say what I want to. Stop trying to change the subject." She yelled, and I shut up and let her finish.

"You have got to stop leading that girl on, the minute you stop feeding into her she'll get some business bout herself. She—" I cut her off.

"You right ma." I said. She looked at me shocked because normally I would let that shit go in one ear and out the other. I wasn't interested in how to make her stop because as long as the pussy was convenient, I was good. Now that I had found somebody that I was interested in I knew that I needed to chill out with her unstable ass.

"Well shit, about time." she said and went back to washing the dishes.

"Ima go and talk to her."

"Talk wit ya damn clothes on Zan."

I laughed because she knew me oh too well. "I got this Tricia."

"Umhmmm." She said under her breath right as there was a knock at the door. I looked at moms to see if she was expecting company. When her facial expression looked just as confused as mine, I knew it could only be one person. "That got damn girl just don't fucking learn," Mama said heading to the door. A part of me wanted to let mama tear her ass a new one, but like she said all of this was my got damn fault, so I stopped her.

"I got this ma." Was all I said and went to the door. I cracked it open and peeped my head out like I was trying to see who it was when I already knew.

"The fuck you want?"

"Why the fuck you ain't answering my fucking phone calls?"

"Did you have my son." She tried to open the door, and I popped her hand. "Back the fuck up Tash."

"Why can't I come in? I know you ain't got that bitch in there?"

"Don't worry about who in my mom's crib, the fuck you want?" I taunted her. I could hear my mama in the background running her damn mouth, but I had this.

"Don't fucking play with me." she threatened.

"You want me to let ma come out here and tell you that shit." she calmed down and let go of the door. I opened the door and stepped to the side to let her in. She rolled her eyes and stepped through the threshold but stopped in her tracks when she saw mama standing there drying off this big ass carving knife.

"H—Hi Mrs. Caldwell." Tasha's normal turn up attitude was gone.

"It's Ms., and you remember what happened last night don't you? Don't come in here with that ratchet shit, this time I won't stop myself." Tasha nodded, and mama walked back in the kitchen. I looked back and forth between her and where mama was standing. What the fuck happened last night that got Tasha acting like this.

"The fuck mama do to you?" I asked her and before she could say anything here come Tricia with her mouth.

"Don't worry about all that, you just do what you need to do." She pointed the knife at me again.

I mugged her short ass, and she turned to go back in the kitchen. I escorted Tasha to the basement where I come to chill when I just need to get away from everything. We got down there Tasha headed straight for the bed, and I had to stop her.

"Nah it ain't even that kinda party, over here." I pointed to the couch, and she smacked her lips. "We need to talk."

"Yeah, we need to talk about you having my son around that bitch." She seethed.

"Stop calling Neala out of her name. That girl ain't did shit to you, you ain't got no reason to be mad with her. If anything yo problem should be with me." I started, and she sat down facing me with her arms crossed across her chest. "Look. First I just want to apologize for—"

"Good yo ass need to apologize for being so damn disrespectful, now all I need to hear is that you ain't gone have him around her no more." She said all in one breath.

"Shut the fuck up and listen. My ass is sitting here trying to be all sentimental and shit and here you go running yo got damn mouth. Got damn the only time you quiet is when a dick is in yo mouth, and you wonder why muthafuckas don't take you seriously." That calm speech was short-lived now I was pissed and was about to give it to her raw and uncut.

"So what you trying to say Zan?"

"I'm saying that I don't want you and I never have, the only reason I fuck with you is because the pussy good and it's convenient, but that's about it. You ain't got shit going for yourself. I don't want to be with nobody that is okay living off the system." I fussed.

"You ain't had a problem with none of that until you met that nappy headed bitch."

"Well that nappy headed bitch done found a place in here." I patted my chest and sighed heavily. "Look, Tash, we gone have to deal with each other because of Z2, but that's it."

"So it's just fuck me?"

"I apologize for my part I played in all of this. I kept fucking you knowing yo ass you was retarded. I knew you didn't understand the fact that I didn't want you but I kept on, and that was my fault. You didn't deserve that, I should have cut off my dick supply a long time ago. I guess that was me being selfish because I knew that you would always be there when I wanted you to be. That shit was wrong, and I can't do you like that anymore."

There was anger mixed with a little bit of hurt in her eyes. I couldn't change the way I felt if I wanted to. I didn't want Tasha, and I never had.

"You will never stop fucking with all of this, and you know it."

"Tasha, you trying to make some forever shit out of what was meant to be a hit and quit. I told you from the beginning that I didn't want you, you know that. You thought that Z2 was gone change that and it didn't."

She ignored me and got up and went and laid on the bed. She was dressed in a red maxi dress that she hiked up and spread her legs. I swallowed hard when she started playing with her pussy. I looked up at the sky and talked myself down, I was better than this and I knew it.

"You telling me you gone give up this wet pussy?"

I walked over to the bed, and she smiled thinking that she had me. I shocked the shit out of her when I shook my head and walked up the stairs. I was proud of myself, that was the first time I had ever passed up on some pussy.

Walking in the kitchen, I sat down on the stool at the bar and grabbed a piece of leftover bacon that she had on a plate. Neala was really starting to get to a nigga, cause I damn sure wouldn't have did that shit for no one else.

"SO?" mama asked, and I shrugged my shoulders. "Don't play with me boy." She said.

"I told her what it was, and she didn't believe me. she laid on the bed and started playing in her shit, I looked at her and walked the hell out." I looked at my mama who was shaking her head. She was used to my honesty, so nothing I said shocked her anymore. If she asked me a question, she was gone get the real answer no matter how bad.

She walked over to where I was sitting, "I'm so proud of you." She hugged me tightly.

"Really ma?" I pushed her off.

"Yeah son, I know who ya daddy is, so I know how hard that was for you." She laughed, but I didn't see shit funny about any of that. She may have been over it, but that shit still affected me til this day, hence the situation that I'm in right now. "Now that all that's over, who is the nappy headed bitch she keeps referring to."

"The one you helped me plan the date for wit yo nosey ass." I laughed, and she joined in. "I'll have to bring her by here to meet you, or better yet she's having an art show next week to show off her shit, you can meet her there."

"Umm an Artist, cultured." She smiled and then looked to the door. I didn't even hear Tasha come back up the stairs.

"Daddy daddy daddy call Nene," Z2 said running in the kitchen where we were making shit all that much worse.

"Who is Nene," mama asked, and Tasha smacked her lips.

"The nappy headed bitch," I said, and mama laughed.

"Well, I can't wait to meet Nene."

Tasha looked at me with tears in her eyes and turned to leave out the door. I knew that she was hurt because she didn't get loud, she wasn't all hype and shit. She didn't say anything, and that wasn't like her.

"Bye mommy." Z2 jumped off my lap and ran to her grabbing her legs, and that's when she let the tears go that were pooling in her eyes.

"Tash—" she held her hand up to stop me, and she picked up Z2 and kissed him on the jaw. She looked back at me one more time and headed out the door. I had a feeling this wasn't gonna be the end of this. But for now, I was gone enjoy it. I talked to mama for a little while, and then me and Z2 headed out for our little date with Neala at Sky Zone. Today was gone be a good day.

KY

When I got back from seeing what the hell was going on with Zan, Asta's ass was sleep. I told her little drunk ass that we needed to talk. The feeling that I felt when I walked in there and saw her smiling all in that niggas face was indescribable. I wanted to wring her neck and take his life, but I knew she was feeling some type of way.

The minute Lovey text me a picture of Asta partying her ass off and getting drunk I automatically knew that she had started some shit. I knew how she operated, her and Tasha were cousins so that should tell you something. They weren't close by a long shot, but they still had the same blood running through them.

I called her after she sent me the third picture and asked her what her angle was and she said that she was just looking out for me because she knew how I felt about Asta. I didn't believe that for one second so I asked her what she said to her and she swore that she never approached her. I knew she was lying, but I let her believe that everything was everything. I even set up a little lunch date with her at Kennedy's, what she didn't know is that Asta would be with me. I was not about to be like Zan's ass, we was getting this shit straight right here and now.

I stripped out of my clothes and laid down behind her. It was as if she sensed I was there because she started to stir until I slip right behind her and put my hand around her waist. She cuddled up with me and began to snore lightly. As bad as I wanted to wake her ass up so we could talk, a nigga was tired, and that shit could wait til in the morning. I kissed Asta on the neck and then drifted off into a peaceful sleep.

I was awakened by the sound of Asta throwing up in the bathroom. It sounded like her ass was about to die. I pulled myself out of bed and went to check on her.

"Bet yo ass won't drink like that no more."

"I ain't never drinking again," she was able to get out before Earl called again.

"Yeah, that's what they all say." I laughed. "The fuck was you drinking?"

"Henny and Patron."

"Together? No wonder you ass sound like death." She flipped me off, and I laughed again. "Ima grab yo ass a Gatorade and some Tylenol. We got shit to do today."

"Nooooooo I just wanna sleep."

"Nah fuck that. First, we gotta lunch date with Lovey," she

snapped her head around so fast that she made herself sick again from the sudden movement. "Chill, that shit she pulled last night wasn't cool, and I wanna make sure that shit don't happen again. I wanna nip this shit in the bud now, so we don't have that problem again, I don't want to come out of retirement but I will." I looked at her, and she turned her head. "And my sister is home from college, so her and my mom is gonna meet us at the restaurant, cause I'm sure Lovey won't be there long. If she is my mom will be sure to run her ass away."

Moms hated Lovey, she told me when she first met her that she wasn't the one for me, but I didn't listen. I just thought she was on that no one is good enough for her baby boy trip but turns out moms was righter than a muthafucka. That was one of the reasons I wanted her to meet Asta, I hoped like hell they got along because I was falling for Asta hard as hell, quick as hell.

"I can't meet your mom like this." She whined.

"Well, you better get yourself together then." I smiled and went to the refrigerator and grabbed her a Gatorade and some Tylenol. She took it and went to lay in the bed. "You gotta get up in like an hour, we gotta be at Kennedy's at one."

"I need an hour nap." She said, and I looked at her.

"I know what you need," I smirked, and she smiled.

"I can't." that whining was making my dick hard.

"You gone make ya man walk around like this?" I grabbed my dick. She tried to sit up, but I guess it made her sick and she ran back in the bathroom and started to throw up again. My dick went limp in a matter of seconds. "Ain't that some shit." I shook my head and went to hold her hair. The shit a nigga do for love.

~

We had just got to the restaurant, and Lovey wasn't there yet. I looked over at Asta, and she cleaned up nice. This morning she was looking like death, but she was sitting beside me looking like she was ready for her movie debut. She had her dreads pulled up in a bun on top of her head just like I liked it; her makeup was light because she didn't really need that shit but let her tell it she did today. She wore a long black and hot pink dress that rode every curve that God blessed her with. I couldn't help but stare at her.

"Babe stop that." She looked at me out of the corn of her eye.

"Shit I can't help it, you look beautiful baby." She leaned over and tried to kiss me, and I leaned back to prevent her from doing so. "You brush yo teeth." She slapped my arm and leaned over to kiss me anyway.

"Yes I did, but if you can't love me at my worst then baby, you don't deserve me at my best."

"The fuck you mean I held yo hair while yo funky ass threw up everywhere." She burst out laughing, so loud that the other patrons looked our way. She stood up and leaned down and kissed me.

"You make me sick, I'll be back I gotta go freshen up. Gotta be on point." She winked playfully, but I knew she meant that shit. Although she didn't have shit to worry about, when I first saw Lovey, I must admit I had a rush of feelings come back but it didn't take me long to remember why she was my ex.

The waitress came over and asked if I wanted to order drinks,

I told her that I was waiting on a few more guests. As she was walking away, I saw Lovey walk in. I had to laugh to myself because she was dressed like she knew that I was leaving with her after this. The short ass navy skirt let me know that she thought she was getting rewarded for her little findings last night.

"Hey, Ky." She said walking over to where I was attempting to kiss me, and I put my hand in front of her mouth to let her know it wasn't this type of party. "Damn this is the thanks that I get?" she snarled up her pretty nose.

"For what, starting a bunch of shit between my lady and me?"

"What are you talking about Ky I—" she stopped mid sentence and I followed her eyes and almost every other eye in here to Asta who had just emerged from the bathroom. "Really Ky?"

"Yeah what you thought this was?" I mugged her and then diverted my attention to the disrespectful muthafuckas watching my woman. "She's taken and if you know what's good for you, you would watch your fucking eyes," I said loud enough for the watchers to direct their attention elsewhere.

"Babe," Asta said with her hands on her hips, not even acknowledging Lovey sitting there. "You need to cut it out."

"Fuck that, I know they saw you sitting here with me. That's disrespectful as fuck."

"Speaking of disrespectful," she turned towards Lovey. "Lovey, is it?" she said being smart. I smirked because I had a feeling this was gone be a short meeting.

"What's this Ky?" Lovey asked me.

"I needed to get some shit off my chest, and I need both of you to be here when I do it." I looked at her, and I saw a twinkle of hope in her eyes and I was about to crush that shit. "First off don't you ever approach my girl off no bullshit again, you know me meeting with you wasn't on no me wanting to get with you because that is not the case and never will be." She opened her mouth and shut it again. "Why do you think that I would want you after you just told me that you hid a whole baby from me."

"Wait, what?" Asta sat up in her seat.

"Oh, you didn't tell your little girlfriend?" I wanted to wipe the fucking smirk off of her face.

"I didn't get to tell my woman anything yet, her drunk ass passed out last night." I looked at Asta, and she bit her bottom lip to show her growing frustration with this conversation. "She was pregnant when she left, but the baby was stillborn." I waited for a response, Asta got up out of her seat and sat in my lap and hugged my neck. The gesture was sincere; I could tell when she looked me in the eyes.

"I'm so sorry to hear that baby, are you okay?"

"Yeah I'm good, I just hate that I didn't even get a chance to feel anything concerning the baby. It's fucked up, but it is what it is. I'll just have to wait until you give me babies." I kissed her lips, and she got up off my lap and returned to her seat.

"I am not about to do this." Lovey stood up.

"Hold up, the whole reason that I called you here was to let you know that this." I motioned between the two of us. "Died a long time ago, so the shit from last night, let that be the last time. Matter of fact there is not one reason you should have to call me because we have no ties. I got the closure that I needed, and I hope you did too. I wish you nothing but the best Lovey but that best ain't with me." I looked her dead in her eyes praying that she caught the drift.

"So I'm just nothing to you?"

"You were nothing when you disappeared and didn't tell me shit." I shrugged. "End of conversation," I added a little bass, so she knew I was over all of this. "Lose my number."

She smacked her lips and stood up right as my mom and sister were coming in. My mom walked up to the table and slammed her pocketbook on the table and stared at Lovey. I know I should have stopped her, but this was a long time coming.

"Just say the word bro and that cheap ass lace front will be wrapped around my hand." Xavia, my little sister, said through clenched teeth.

"Chill X." was all I said.

"What is she doing here?" my mother said looking at me.

"Oh, she was just leaving." Asta smiled and stood up. "Hi, I'm Asta." She greeted my mom and sister who was very receptive to her introduction.

"Bye." Moms turned to look at Lovey who was looking at the exchange with envy in her eyes. She never had a relationship with my mother and sister. She looked at me and smacked her lips grabbed her purse and stomped off. I was hoping that was the last time I saw her. "Son she's pretty." Moms beamed. "So tell me about my daughter in law, because if Ky is bringing you to meet me it gots to be something special." I smiled at her and watched as the three ladies talked and got to know each other.

This just made everything that much more real. I got my three favorite women in one place and they talking and laughing like they've known each other for years. This was it, Asta was it."

RONDO

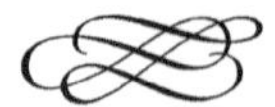

Char and I had been really trying to get our shit together lately, and I was happy as hell that she was actually putting in the effort to fix shit. She was no longer throwing that shit in my face although I knew that the shit was still lingering in the back of her mind. I could tell because whenever we would talk about kids or the future, she would get this far away look in her eyes.

Rachel was trying her little shit every now and then, but she knew only to go so far. I did my best to keep Char away from it, and until now I was doing a damn good job. Today she called and said that she thought that she was in labor while me and Char was getting ready for the race we had today.

"So you going to the hospital."

"Nah, what the fuck I need to go to the hospital for? I ain't no doctor. She can call me when it's time for the DNA, and I will take my test. If the baby comes back to be mine, I will set up child support and visitation." I shrugged, to me, it was that simple, and there was no need to discuss anything else.

"You think she gone let shit be just like that?" Char smirked like she knew something I didn't.

"What choice does she have Char?"

"You think that if you want to, she is gonna have more power over you than you think." She chuckled. "Look at Zan's ass.

I thought about all the shit he was going through since he stopped fucking with Tasha. She had fucked up his car and busted the windows out of his house. She had the police called on him one day when he went and got Z2. IF it weren't for Z2, his ass would have been in jail for domestic abuse. Z2 told the cops that his mama was ignorant, which I'm sure he got from Zan's dumb ass, and that he didn't hit mommy. After questioning Tasha a few more times, she finally told the cop they were just in a custody battle.

"I will kill that bitch first." I shook my head just thinking about that shit. My phone rang, and I looked down at it, and it was Rachel again. I cleared and went back to getting my bike set to race. I was over all the bull shit, I just needed to know if the baby was mine.

"Answer the phone Ron; something could be wrong." The sadness in her voice made not want to answer the phone even more, but when it rang again, I answered it.

"What?"

"Why do you have to be so mean? I just wanted to let you know that they are taking the baby."

"Ain't it too early?" if they were taking the baby now it was a great chance that it wasn't mine.

"Yeah it is, they said he'll probably be in the NICU for a while. He's only four pounds, I'm so scared." She cried and I kind of felt bad for her. "Can you come?"

"Come where?"

"To the hospital Rondo, I don't want to go through this by myself."

"I'm sorry but until I know if it's my baby or not I'm not doing shit. I already told you that."

"You know Ryan is in jail and he can't be here," she yelled. After the night he broke into the palace the police got him on some heavy ass drug charges. They didn't even give his ass a bond, he was waiting on his trial date.

"That shit ain't got nothing to do with me. Call me when the baby is here so I can take my test, and if the baby is mine, we will set up our arrangements."

"Arrangements?"

"Yeah, child support and visitation." I could hear her breathing on the phone, but she didn't say anything else. I was about to ask her if there was anything else but I heard her click off the line. I didn't know who she thought I was or what she wanted from me but this was all I had to give until that test said otherwise. "Fuck it."

"I was afraid of this," Char said as she looked down at her phone and then back up at me.

"Baby, please don't do this we talked about this." I pleaded with her.

"I know we did baby, and I'm trying, but the reality is this woman is giving you something that only I'm supposed to give you. I can say I'm gonna be okay with it, and it's not gonna bother me but that shit is easier said than done."

I reached out and pulled her to me and kissed her on the forehead. I already had it in my mind that this may affect our relationship no matter how much we say that it wouldn't. I knew it would, how could it not? But I was gone try my best to not let this shit destroy us.

"I love you." I kissed her lips.

"I love you too, now go win me some money yo ass owe me a damn vacation." She tried to play off her feelings, but I knew better.

She walked off to the bleachers with Asta and Neala. I was glad that she found friendship in them. They were all getting so close, and it helped her through some of the shit that she was going through with me and she needed that. The fact that she had someone to talk about how she felt with she couldn't tell me was beneficial, even though I hated them knowing my business, but if it helps Char, I was good.

I headed over to where Zan and Ky were at, and Zan had a mug on his face. I didn't even want to ask what happened now. I told his ass that fucking with that girl was come back to bite him in the ass, we all did now look. She was making his life hell.

"The fuck you looking like you ready to murder some damn body for?"

"Cause I'm about to," he said through clenched teeth. "I

fucking hate Tasha, and if she comes here on some shit, I swear I'm going to jail." I knew he meant every word he said.

"What happened now?" Ky asked.

"The bitch just sent me a picture of Neala's house, and she had busted out the windows."

"Oooohhhh." Me and Ky both put our fist up to our mouths and said.

"Tell me about it, her angry little ass gone flip the fuck out," he said and dropped his head. It was funny to see Zan worried about how a woman was gone act, he never gave a fuck about shit, to be honest. Neala had that nigga planning dates and shit, doing all types of shit he don't normally do. I liked that shit for him though, it calmed his dumb ass down some.

"You gone tell her."

"Nigga I ain't got no choice, that's where we were staying tonight. All Z2 shit over there." he dropped his head, and the phone went off again. "Got damn it that's it." he tried to walk off, but Ky grabbed him.

"Chill nigga." He was trying not to laugh. "Let me see." He grabbed the phone, and he got pissed himself. "My nigga kill that bitch." He said and passed his phone back.

"Nah don't listen to Ky's hostile ass. What the fuck." I grabbed the phone and his brand-new Cadillac Escalade was decorated with the words "Dog ass nigga" in bright red, there were no windows left and from the looks of the way the car was sitting one or more of his tires were flat. "Bruh."

"Exactly, I hope Neala's nosey ass neighbors seen that shit and reported her ass. Fuck this shit I gotta race." He hopped on his bike and headed to the start line. I felt bad for my nigga but we all tried to tell his ass, and he didn't listen. I was praying I didn't have to deal with that shit if this baby was mine. I don't think I could handle that shit at all.

"You ready to go make this money?" Ky asked.

"Yeah, my nigga, and then we got to go with this nigga to straighten out this shit." Ky shook his head and put on his helmet. I did the same and rode down to where the races were about to begin. This was gone be a long ass day I just knew it.

ZAN

My day started out so got damn good, I had my woman and my son with me. Shit was great until ignorant ass Tasha started doing dumb shit. After that little talk at my mama house I thought she was just gone leave shit alone and for a while she did. I would go and pick Z2 up, and she wouldn't even say nothing to me, she would get his bag and send him on his way. She even went out and got a got damn job, I was low key proud of her.

Things were going so good then all of a sudden it was like a light switch went off, and she started on her shit again. She quit her job and started calling me all times a night and when I wouldn't answer she would text and threaten to come where I was. Whenever I would go see what the fuck she wanted, it was always on some bullshit and never about our son.

The fact that I was sticking to my word and not fucking with her anymore was driving her ass crazy. Now y'all see why I fucked with her ass to keep the peace. Tash was on some other shit now, fucking with Neala shit was a no no. So far all of her little tactics were towards me, I pushed her around a couple of times behind that shit, but it seemed to only make shit worse. I didn't know how I was gone explain this shit to Neala ass, she gone swear I'm back fucking her when in reality I ain't. A nigga been good.

"Aye, bruh, clear yo got damn head and be safe," Ky said rolling up behind me. I nodded and tried to relax but I was pissed, and I couldn't control it, so I was gone have to take that shit out on the blacktop.

"Go Daddy." I heard and looked up, and Neala had Z2 on her shoulders, and they were cheering and pointing at me.

I think my got damn heart smiled for the first time in my life. Why couldn't life just be this simple? I wish like hell I would have just met Neala first and none of this would be happening right now.

The announcer prompted us to roll forward, I looked over at my competition, and he was a young cat probably just starting to ride. He wasn't wearing colors, which was weird, it was rare that we got independent cats racing in the legit races. Big money had to be paid to get in these races, but here he was. I wasn't complaining because I didn't discriminate I'd take anybody's money.

We rolled to the line, and I watched as the light turned yellow then green. I took off on my opponent and gassed that bitch. I was in my groove until I saw ol' boy roll up on me. I turned it up a notch just in time to hit the finish line. I rolled off to a good stop and then I turned around to where ol' boy was.

"Nigga you can ride." I dapped him up.

"You too homie, I just knew I had you." He had the nerve to say.

"Shit, you ain't that good," I smirked, and he laughed. "What's ya name?"

"Wood."

"Who you wit?"

"You the third person that has asked me that, I'm with myself. That's how we ride in New York." I knew he wasn't from here the minute he started talking. That accent was a dead give away.

"That's what's up, what part of New York you from?"

"New York, New York baby." I nodded, and his eyes went to something behind me which made me turn around real quick. "Who is that?" he pointed in the direction of Asta, Neala, Char, and Xavia.

"Don't worry about none of them." I went ahead and let him know that all of them were off limits.

"I know her." he pointed.

"Bruh you don't know them." I hopped back on my bike and was about to head in the direction of Neala and the girls.

"Xavia?" he called out, and she froze. She looked from him to me and then turned around and took off running in the opposite direction. "Xavia! Is that you?" he tried to take off after her, and I stopped him.

"Nah bruh that's little sis can't let you do that." I was defensive as hell because I didn't know this nigga but he knew X, she was Ky sister which made her my sister. He looked at me and then in the direction that Xavia went. I couldn't quite read his facial expression, but I was damn sure gone holla at sis about what that was about. "I'll holla at cha." I got back on my bike and rolled off.

I met up with Neala and Z2 to wait for Rondo and Ky to finish so I could get the fuck out of here and go deal with the shit my dumb ass baby mama had done. I hated that bitch with a passion. She better pray that I don't get my hands on her.

This bike fest was the last thing on my mind right now. I was mentally preparing to tell Neala what the fuck happened to her house and my car that was parked in front of her house. I didn't know how she was gone take this at all. She looked so happy running through the parking lot with Z2, it was shame that I was gone have to ruin all that shit.

"Hello?" I heard her say on the phone. "Say what?" I heard her screech, and I knew it one of her nosey ass neighbors called to tell her before I could. Fuck! She hung up the phone and walked towards me. "Do you know what ya baby mama been doing today?" she was calm, and it was scary.

"Yeah."

"Yeah? You knew about this shit? When the fuck were you gone tell me."

"Oooohhhh Nene mad," Z2 said watching the exchange between the two of us. She leaned down and kissed his cheek and rubbed his head and he laughed.

"I was about to tell you now."

“I told you I was not about to deal with this shit Zan I don’t want nothing to do with any of this.”

“I know baby that’s why shit been cool, I handled it. I don’t know what the fuck her problem is all of a sudden.” I shook my head, and she tilted hers to the side. I already knew what she was thinking. “Don’t even fucking think it,” I warned her.

“Well there has to be a reason for her to be acting all stupid again, I mean shit was all good and now boom! I mean unless you just now leaving the bitch alone. Which one is it Zan.”

“It’s fucking neither, the night after the fucking club after you said what you had to say I cut that shit off. I did what the fuck you asked me to do. I ain’t got to lie about shit. You know good, and damn well if I was still fucking the bitch, I would have no problem telling you that.” I had to catch myself because I was taking my frustrations out on her and I knew that she had every right to think that. “My bad baby, but no I ain’t fucked with her since before that night, and I put that on my life.”

She didn’t say anything she just looked at me and nodded her head. I didn’t know if she believed me or not but it was the truth, and there was nothing else I could say about it. WE got in the car, and I shot Ky and Rondo a text letting them know that I was gone go ahead and head out. They were still down there collecting money and shit. I didn’t have time to wait if her neighbors were calling her that means they were all out there being nosey as fuck.

We hopped in the car and pulled out. When we got to the house, I could see Neala’s face turn beet red. She was pissed the fuck off, and she had every right to be. I didn't know how to comfort her right now because I was just as mad.

"Look at this shit!" she screamed and walked around her house. "Who takes time out of their fucking day to do some shit like this."

I wondered where her nosey ass neighbors when she was doing this shit in broad ass daylight. But they called saying that they saw the shit. I went straight to my car and looked at it, my paint job was all fucked up, the bitch even fucked up my interior. If I got my hands on the bitch, I was gone hurt her. My phone rang it was Ky.

"Bruh you seen X?"

"No, that nigga I was racing knew her ass from school I guess cause he was from New York too. She seen him and took off, I ain't seen her since."

"I'm calling her ass and she ain't answering." He said sounding worried. I was about to say something, but I heard a car pull up.

"Who's the bitch now." Was all I heard before gunshots erupted. My first instinct was to run and protect my son and Neala, but she had him on the ground covering him. I was trying my best to get over there when I felt a bullet pierce my back and I fell to the ground. I could hear Ky yelling my name through the phone that was still in my hand and tires screeching.

"Somebody help! Call 911!" Neala yelled and ran over to where I was. I could hear Z2 crying, but I couldn't get to him. I could barely keep my eyes open. "Zan baby open your eyes, you gotta open your eyes. Stay with me, baby. Oh God! Somebody help me somebody help!" I could feel her tears falling on my face. It was getting harder and harder to stay woke.

"I love you."

"Baby I love you stay woke. Somebody help me." I could hear the sirens coming, but it was too late. I closed my eyes, I was too weak to fight it anymore. The last thing I heard was Neala screaming. "Zannnnnnn!"

KY

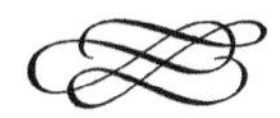

I could hear the gun shots through the phone, I called out to Zan, but he didn't say anything. I could hear Neala crying out, and I just kept yelling through the phone.

"Neala! Neala! Neala! What the fuck is going on?" I yelled.

"What's up Ky," Rondo said coming over to where I was.

"Some shit just went down at Neala house, all I heard was gunshots and Neala screaming," I said frantically. I put the phone back up to my ear. "Neala talk to me, sis." I pleaded and then all of a sudden, I heard my nephew on the phone.

"KyKy."

"Hey nephew," I tried to calm down enough to not alarm him. "Where's daddy?"

"Daddy asleep, wake up daddy wake up." He said and I could feel my heart drop to my stomach. "He no wake up."

"It's okay Uncle Ky coming okay?" I told him.

"Nene uncle Ky coming." He told Neala, and I guess she snapped out of her trance because she came on the phone.

"Oh God Ky come quick somebody shot Zan." She cried.

"Who shot him?" I was seething by this point, and Rondo was headed to his car and Asta was pulling me in the direction of where they were headed. I was in no position to drive.

"I DON'T KNOW!" She screamed so loud that I had to take the phone away from my ear. My blood was boiling and I was ready to take a life. If my brother died the city of Charlotte was gone feel my pain, every fucking drop of it.

"I'm on my way." was all I said and then I hung up the phone I couldn't take her crying. It was fucking me up all the way. "Somebody shot Zan." I could feel the tears stinging my eyes. I didn't cry much, but right now I didn't give a fuck who saw me.

"He's gonna be okay." Asta said and climbed in my lap, we were in the back of Rondo's Tahoe. I wrapped my arms around her, buried my face in her neck and I cried like I had never cried before.

When we pulled up to Neala's house I saw the paramedics working on him in the yard. I walked up to them to see what the fuck they were doing and why they hadn't taking him to the hospital yet.

"Why the fuck y'all still out here, take my nigga to a fucking hospital." I screamed and Rondo pulled me back.

"Chill nigga."

"Fuck that get him the fuck out of here." I screamed on them again and Neala broke down crying with my nephew in her arms. "Got him out here watching this the fuck wrong with y'all."

It only took them a few minutes to finally get him on a gurney and get him to a hospital. I got a good look at each one of them because if he died they were gonna be on my hit list too. We got Neala under control and followed the ambulance to the hospital. They rushed him in for surgery.

I paced the waiting room, they kept telling me to calm down and sit down but I couldn't. My fucking brother was in there fighting for his life and I couldn't take that shit. How in the hell was I supposed to explain to his son if he didn't make it, I needed that nigga to pull through.

I felt Asta's arms around my waist and I embraced it. "He's gonna be okay, You gotta believe that." she said and I nodded and she stood on her tiptoes and kissed my lips. "I love you."

"I love you too, go be with your sister, she ain't doing to good." I nodded over there to Neala who was rocking back and forth in a chair by the door.

"What happened to my baby." I heard Ma Tricia say the minute she rounded the corner. She was already crying. I had Rondo call her because I couldn't, I didn't have it in me. "Is he gonna be okay?" she asked.

"They haven't told us shit ma," I said leaning down to kiss her.

"How did this happen Ky?" I dropped my head, I couldn't even answer her. I should have been with him, I knew I shouldn't have let him go by himself, but I was looking for my sister.

"Tasha dumb ass broke out all the windows in Neala house and then fucked up his car, so he took off from the track to go see what all the fuck she did. I was on my way because I didn't want him to go after her, but I was looking for my sister. She got missing and we couldn't find her.

"So that bitch did this." Ma got amped.

"We don't know Neala was around the house looking at the damage done to her house when she heard the gun shots." I put my head down.

"Oh Neala." I was like she remembered that she was there. "Is she okay." she asked me and I shook my head no, she wasn't okay and if something happened to him I didn't know what she would do. Her last boyfriend died, and it was like history was repeating itself. "Don't blame yourself, this wasn't on you." She kissed my cheek and went to comfort Neala.

"We need to find out who did this shit."

"I'm ready to make this fucking city bleed," I said through gritted teeth.

"Oh, my God oh my God oh my God." I heard someone screaming coming around the corner. When I saw it was Tasha, I immediately grabbed my piece and met her when she entered the waiting room. My gun immediately went to her head. "Ky please," she cried.

"Did you do this?" With every tear that fell from my eyes that angrier I got. I was ready to kill somebody, and I didn't give a fuck if it was in the hospital and I didn't give a fuck who was around.

"No Ky you got to believe me, I wouldn't do no shit like that."

"If I find out you had anything to do with my brother laying on that operating table I swear you gone hate the day you spread yo rotten ass pussy for him." she was crying so hard she had snot running from her nose. "Now get the fuck out of here, bitch you ain't family." I lowered my gun.

"My son's here, and that's my baby daddy in there." she grew some balls I chambered a bullet and pointed my gun back at her head.

"What the fuck I say," I growled.

She looked around, and she and Neala locked eyes before I could even react Neala was on top of her beating the shit out of her. I was so shocked because I saw Neala fuck her up one time but got damn she was like the Tasmanian devil up in this bitch. I put my gun up and tried to break that shit up before security came in here trying to put people out and cause a bigger problem.

"Neala let her go," I said as I tried to pull her away, but Neala had her weave wrapped around her hand and wasn't trying to let go.

"Family of Zander Caldwell," the doctor said as he entered the waiting room looking around. I can only imagine what the fuck he was thinking. After hearing the doctor's voice, Neala reluctantly let go of Tasha. We all walked towards him, and he looked around the room. "I have good news and bad news." He started, and I ran my hands down my face to try and calm down I needed to know what the fuck was going on and now, fuck the bullshit. "We were able to remove the bullet; it missed his spine by four centimeters. The bad news is he's slipped into a coma, we did a CT scan, and it shows brain activity, so it's up to him to wake up." He told us.

The room fell silent because we were all trying to grasp what the doctor had just said, I didn't know what to think. I was glad he made it through, but I needed that nigga to wake the fuck up. I needed him out here on these streets with me.

"Nooooooo!" we heard as Neala broke down again. I can only imagine how she felt. Asta and Ma Tricia ran to her side and Tasha's bitch as just looked on in envy. Something was telling me that she knew something about this and if I found out she did, only God himself would be able to protect her from what I had coming.

About two hours later they came back and told us that we could come back and see him three at a time. Me, ma Tricia and Neala went back first. Asta kept Z2 with her. When we walked in Neala started to cry.

"Sis, you good? Maybe you should just wait."

"No, I'm gone be right here." she glared at me. She went and grabbed a chair and slid it right on the side of the bed. Sat down and laid her head on his arm. "I'm not leaving this spot until you wake up!" she said talking to Zan. "And don't be an asshole and stay sleep just see how long I will sit here either. I know you, Zander." She said and then stood up to kiss his lips. The monitor that was monitoring his heart sped up, and she smiled. "I love you too, now wake yo ass up." She said.

I spoke my peace and then went back to the waiting room to let everyone else come back. Neala and Ma Tricia refused to leave, so I did. After everyone left, Ma Tricia came out and grabbed Z2 and took him with her. She said she needed to be close to Zan and Z2 was the closest thing. I had to go back in there and see my nigga one more time.

"Aye, nigga wake yo ass up. We got to put in some work. You just being fucking lazy." I looked at all the tubes coming out of him and all the shit connected to him, and a nigga got choked up. Asta came up beside me and grabbed my hand. "I know yo ass don't want me to go, Rambo, I'll be somewhere locked the hell up. So get the fuck up!" I said and then stared at him like he was gone all of a sudden wake up at my command. I let a few more tears drop. "Who ever did this gone pay for every tear that fell, nigga." I balled his hand into a fist and dapped him up. "I love you bruh."

I walked over and kissed Neala and Asta gave her a hug and told her to call us if she needs us. She told us she would. I grabbed Asta's hand, and we headed to my house. I prayed to God that he forgave me for what I was about to do. These mutha-fuckas ain't even gone know what's coming.

CHAR

It had been two weeks, and Zan still hadn't woke up. Rondo and Ky were running around the town like wild animals trying to figure out who the fuck did it. Everybody was scared as fuck to be around their psycho asses. I just prayed that he woke up soon or these two were gonna go crazy.

"Knock knock," I said slowly pulling the door open to Zan's hospital room.

"Hey, girl," Neala said putting Vaseline on Zan's lips.

"How's he doing?"

"The same," she half smiled. "His vitals are good, and he has a lot of brain activity, we're just waiting on him."

"Are you okay?" she looked tired, more than usual.

"I'm pregnant." She smiled. "I just found out yesterday, I told his ass if he didn't wake the fuck up I was going to get an abortion." She said, and the monitors started going crazy, and she laughed for the first time in weeks. "It does that every time I say that. Sometimes I say it just to make sure he's listening." She sighed and sat down beside him; she rubbed her nonexistent stomach. "I need him to wake up, I miss his aggravating ass."

"Well, at least you won't go through being pregnant alone." It was my turn to smile big.

"What?" she gasped. "Really?" I nodded my head. "I'm so happy for you Char, wait you are happy, right?"

"It's bittersweet," I got choked up. "Bitter because Rondo is waiting for his results for the paternity test, sweet because this is everything that I ever wanted and I'm passed the twelve-week scare mark." I squealed. "The doctor thinks that I should be able to carry this one."

I couldn't contain my happiness. I was so excited that I was finally going to get the baby that I always wanted. The only bad part is that I may not be the only one to give Rondo one. I tried not to think about that because the doctor told me to stay stress-free.

"But enough about that, I just left from the doctor, so I wanted to stop by and check you out. I'm about to go share the good news with this man."

"Okay girl call me and let me know what he says."

"Okay boo let us know if anything changes." She nodded her head, and I kissed her, and I left. I headed home to share the good news with Rondo.

I didn't know how he was gone take the news; I hoped he would be happy about it. He has been stressing ever since he took the test for Rachel's baby. I was trying to prepare myself for if that baby was his but I just couldn't find a way to do that. I didn't know what I would do if that was my reality.

I pulled up in the drive way and took out the envelope with the sonogram in it. I looked in the mirror and checked my makeup. It was flawless as usual. Getting out of the car at the same time the mail man was pulling up. I went out and met him so that he wouldn't have to walk up to the house seeing as though our mail box was connected to the house instead of out by the road.

After I got the mail, I made my way to the house and handed the stack to Rondo who began to go through it. For some reason, I got nervous and ran to the bathroom to relieve my stomach contents. Once I had myself together, I walked back in the living room, and Rondo had some mail out, and he was reading it. He clearly didn't like what it said. He put his head in his hands.

"Baby what's wrong." Then I realized that I put the sonogram and the papers from the doctor in the with the rest of the mail. Maybe he seen and it and he's upset. I walked over to where he was and snatched what he was reading out of his hands. I read the contents of the letter, and my heart dropped to my stomach. The tears fell from my eyes as I read the contents of the letter out loud. "In the case of Rymere Rondo Meeks you are 99.9999999% the father."

To Be Continued…

ALSO BY NIKKI BROWN

Nikki Brown's Catalog

✨Messiah and Reign 1-3

✨I Won't Play A Fool For You (Messiah and Reign spinoff)

✨My Love And His Loyalty 1-3

✨I Deserve your love 1-3

✨Bury My Heart 1-2

✨Beautiful Mistake 1-3

✨Beautiful Revenge

✨Riding Hard For A Thug 1-3

✨You're The Cure To The Pain He Caused

✨Key To The Heart Of A Boss 1-3

✨I Got Love For A Carolina Hustla 1-3

✨A Hood Love Like No Other (Coming 6/25)

CPSIA information can be obtained
at www.ICGtesting.com
Printed in the USA
LVHW09s1944260918
591451LV00001B/42/P